Praise for *Just East of Nowhere*

"From its absorbing first pages, *Just East of Nowhere* is fast paced and tautly written, with the atmospheric pungency of hardscrabble Maine. Better yet is its narrative of complex characters trapped in a chain of miscalculation, mischance, and fateful silences, headed by a sensitive but troubled young man whose search for a father reveals a terrible secret. This is a terrific novel."
—Richard North Patterson, *New York Times* bestselling author

"*Just East of Nowhere* is a spare and observant coming-of-age story that Scot Lehigh has imbued with a strangely timeless quality, one with the resonance of allegory. Young Danny Winters, college student and criminal, stands at the threshold of adulthood, immobilized by the tension between his past and present, drawn home for his mother's wake. Returned to his small hometown of Eastport, we feel the powerful echo of past eras, of past generations who struggled similarly to take their measure in the stark and narrow confines of what they know weighed against all that they don't. Lehigh's leanly plotted debut is warmed by his empathy and the deep familiarity of lived experience, gifting us a propulsive and sharply characterized tale that for all of its suspense holds the stillness of profundity."
—Alexander Parsons, author of *In the Shadows of the Sun*

"Scot Lehigh's novel *Just East of Nowhere* is a haunting and intricately plotted tale of growing up poor on the rugged coast of Maine with nowhere else to go. The frustration of Lehigh's characters is palpable, and the book builds to an explosive ending."
—William F. Weld, former Governor of Massachusetts and author of *Stillwater*

"Every page of *Just East of Nowhere* is a big surprise. There's no predicting what anyone will do because there are no black or white hats. Everyone is a wriggling, writhing critter of complexity and life is a full-blown storm at sea."
—Carolyn Chute, author of *The Beans of Egypt, Maine*

"These Mainers know something about hard knocks and what it takes to confront one's own demons. Lehigh's characters will break your heart."
—Richard Hawke, author of *House of Secrets*

JUST EAST

OF

NOWHERE

A Novel

JUST EAST

OF

NOWHERE

A Novel

Scot Lehigh

ISLANDPORT PRESS

ISLANDPORT PRESS

Islandport Press
P.O. Box 10
Yarmouth, Maine 04096
www.islandportpress.com
info@islandportpress.com

First Edition: July 2023
Printed in the United States of America.

ISBN: 978-1-952143-57-1
eBook ISBN: 978-1-952143-73-1
Library of Congress Control Number: 2022948366

Dean L. Lunt | Editor-in-Chief, Publisher
Emily A. Boyer | Cover Designer
Emily A. Lunt | Book Designer
Author Photo by Kim Case

This is a work of fiction. Names, characters, places, and incidents either are the product of the author's imagination or are used fictitiously. Any resemblance to actual events or persons, living or dead, is entirely coincidental. CONTENT WARNING: This book contains scenes and language which some readers may find offensive or disturbing. Reader discretion is strongly advised. The thoughts, actions, and/or beliefs of the fictional characters in this book do not portray the thoughts, actions, and/or beliefs of the author or the publisher.

To my father, George Lehigh, who passed away on October 1, 2022. After his death I was touched by the notes my family received from his former students, many of whom said he instilled in them a lifelong love of reading. When he was 43, he resettled our family in Eastport, Maine, a place where he felt truly at home and loved for the rest of his life.

PART ONE

CHAPTER 1

THE GREYHOUND SHUDDERED to a stop at Perry Corner, air brakes groaning and hissing.

The driver watched as he carried his pack down the aisle.

"Anything underneath?"

"Nope."

"Have a good one."

"You too."

The bus lumbered away, trailing dust and the smell of diesel. It was seven miles to Eastport. If there had been a cab, he would have gladly paid, but of course there wasn't, not in a place as remote as Perry, so he slung the pack onto his shoulders and trudged back to the turnoff for Route 190.

He considered walking, just to keep his back to the oncoming cars, but that would take the better part of two hours. He heard a car, turned, stuck his thumb out. He could see both driver and passenger looking him over. The car passed. Had it sped up, or was that just him?

A second vehicle approached, slowed, passed, and then a third, as he stood there, thumb extended, smiling benignly. When the last was gone, he turned and started ambling, counting off ten telephone poles before he pivoted and tried again.

He had made it halfway to the Passamaquoddy Reservation before a car finally pulled over. He dropped his pack in the back of the rusting Ford Taurus and settled in next to the driver, a man in his mid-forties with disheveled salt-and-pepper hair and a gut that rolled his faded Red Sox T-shirt down over the waist of his jeans.

"It's Dan, right?"

"Yeah."

"Peter McKinney. Remember me?"

He did, all too well. McKinney was one of Eastport's biggest gossips, asking prying questions and dispensing lewd tittle-tattle along with endless bits of small-town flotsam and jetsam from behind the counter of a convenience store that was a regular stop for the town's nighttime car-cruising crowd.

"Used to work at Stanhope's?"

"Still do. Not much changes around here."

"I guess not."

"Haven't seen you in ages."

"I haven't been back in ages."

"You had some trouble. With Griff Kimball. Gave him quite a thumping."

Dan stared straight ahead.

"I was minding my own business until he started being a fucking jerk, showing off for his asshole friend Sonny Beal and that loser Jimmy Emery."

The road looped up over the nub of a hill and down through Pleasant Point, the Passamaquoddy Tribe's reservation, where squat brick homes sat like Monopoly houses on narrow lots. The wind-stirred sea was a flecked and fretted gray under low-hanging clouds. On the rocky beach, a boy was tossing a Frisbee for his dog, and he watched as the mutt chased after it.

"They sent you away somewhere."

The dog leapt and caught the Frisbee in his mouth, then bounded joyfully around the boy, refusing to give it up.

"But I guess you're out now."

"I broke out."

McKinney's head jerked toward him.

"You're shitting me."

He shifted his own gaze from the herring weirs dotting the cause-way shoreline and looked pointedly out over the bay.

"I'm heading to Canada. I need somebody to take me across. You got a boat?"

"Nope."

"Know anyone who does? I got four hundred bucks. You get half, as a finder's fee. But I gotta go tonight."

"Jesus Christ. They'll be looking for you."

"They won't take me alive." He glanced pointedly toward his pack. "So, can you hook me up with somebody?"

McKinney's eyes darted to him and then back to the road. He gave a quick shake of his head.

"Can't help you there. I'll drop you in town, anywhere you want. But if you get caught, we never had this conversation, okay?"

They had started down the long straight stretch toward Quoddy Village, an outlying residential cluster built to house workers for a massive tidal power project, whose abandonment in the mid-1930s was a grievance that old-timers still nursed against the federal government.

"Actually, I'm at Bates now."

"Bates?"

"Bates College."

"So you're not on the run?"

"No. I've been out for a while."

"Damn, you had me. Hook, line, and sinker." McKinney forced a laugh. "Good one. So I guess you've really turned yourself around."

"I'm trying to be a credit to my people."

If his acid undertone registered, the driver didn't show it.

"That's good. Everybody makes mistakes."

"Yeah." And what about you, he wanted to scream—what about your whole fucking life, your shitty rusting car, your fat-bellied slump, your nowhere job? What are you if not one huge fucking cosmic mistake?

"You must be glad to be getting back, anyway."

"Not really."

"Why's that?"

"I'm here because my mother died."

"Oh, Jesus. I hadn't heard."

He thought of asking how a person who probably jawed with a

tenth of the town each day from his post behind the convenience-store counter could miss the news that one of its 1,600 residents had died. Had his mother really been that insignificant?

"How'd it happen?"

"Car accident."

"Where?"

"Up in Robbinston."

McKinney shook his head, apparently to signal sympathy.

"She was from Lubec originally, right?"

Dan nodded.

"Are you going to bury her over there?"

"No. She considered Eastport her home."

"I guess the church really took her in when she first came and made her one of them."

"I guess."

McKinney ran his hands through his hair and scratched the back of his neck.

"Kind of out there, aren't they?"

Dan responded with a look he hoped signaled puzzlement.

They drove by the Family Dollar store and McKinney navigated the Taurus around the curve and onto Washington Street.

"I mean in a holy-roller-ish way."

"Oh."

"You're not one of . . ."

They passed St. Joseph's, Eastport's sole Catholic church.

"Can you let me off at the next corner?"

He got out onto the gravelly street and grabbed his pack from the backseat.

"Thanks for the lift."

He closed the door before McKinney could reply.

CHAPTER 2

HE WALKED UP the steep High Street hill to the school. It was late in the afternoon now, but there were half a dozen kids out front and he could see that basketball practice, most likely junior varsity, was under way in the gym.

The doors weren't locked. He opened one and stepped inside.

Two squads of teenagers, one in Shead High T-shirts, the others shirtless, were scrimmaging on the far half-court. A skinny point guard tried to set up a play from the top of the key. The ball went around the perimeter in a series of crisp passes but without anyone finding a way to work it inside. Finally, a Native American boy rose from the crouch of a dribble and launched a shot that swished through the net.

A whistle blew.

"Good shot, Ronnell, but Larry, Dean, you guys have got to get open underneath. That's where you get the percentage shots. And the fouls. So set some picks! Okay, skins' ball."

Now the play changed direction, and the two teams came running his way. He watched them scrimmage for ten minutes or so, then slipped back through the double doors and into the chilly afternoon.

A car approached from down High Street hill and stopped in front of the school. A police car. The driver's window dropped.

"What's your business here?" Neither the voice nor the face was familiar.

"I'm just walking."

"Were you in the gym just now?"

He nodded.

"Why?"

"Just wanted to look inside."

"Practices are closed."

He stood mute.

"You're Dan Winters, right?"

"Yeah."

"Well, you need to leave the school premises."

"I wasn't doing anything."

"A word to the wise, Dan. I know your mother has passed. But watch your step while you're in town."

"What's that supposed to mean?"

"It means, do as I say and remove yourself from the premises. Or we'll be taking a ride to the station. Are we clear?" He took a deep breath and held it for a few seconds, then exhaled slowly.

"Yeah."

Turning away from the cruiser, he started north along High Street.

Sooner or later, he had to go to the house. He was going to stay there, after all. He didn't have the money to squander on the Hotel East, as the town's one squat and boxy motel grandly called itself, let alone any of the pricier B&Bs.

But not yet. Now he just wanted to walk.

CHAPTER 3

HIS ANGER HAD receded some by the time he reached the water-front. He followed the paved walk along the harbor's edge until he found a spot where he could sit unobserved on the riprap and watch the breakwater, which served as Eastport's aquatic town square. The long L extended about two hundred feet out into the bay, then turned 90 degrees and ran for four hundred feet parallel to the shore. Dozens of lobster boats and scallop draggers, most bleeding rust and needing paint, were tied up in its lee.

A spin through Eastport inevitably included a slow drive out on the breakwater to see who else was around. It was also an evening meeting spot for the town's teens, a place to park and chat and smoke and drink as you watched another small-town night unfold.

He walked its length, measuring it against memory. The pier was a landmark in his long struggle to break free. Not of Eastport. That hadn't seemed possible, not back then. But of the crimped and narrow place where life had put him.

In a roundabout way, he had the harbor seals to thank for that. During Old Home Week, Eastport's five-day Fourth of July celebration, the breakwater was a people magnet, and on this particular day, he had noticed a group of tourists gathered on the weather side, staring down. Going over to look, he saw a couple of seals frolicking a hundred feet or so out in the bay, their brown bodies swift darting lines in the azure water.

A woman to his left with the bright, spa-tended look of well-off middle age suddenly bent forward, swinging her arm in a swooping arc.

"Oh, damn. My sunglasses."

"You have another pair, don't you?" the man next to her said.

"They're my prescription Armanis."

They were visible there in the water but already starting to sink. He stripped off his T-shirt, kicked off his sneakers, and dove.

The ocean was shockingly cold, so cold it almost burned. He let his momentum carry him down for a second, then stroked twice to pull himself deeper. But where . . . there they were, five feet above him, silhouetted by the sun as they drifted slowly downward. Cradling them in his left hand, he swam to the nearest of the breakwater's round-runged ladders and climbed up.

"Here you go."

The woman smiled gratefully at him.

"What's your name?"

"Dan."

"Well, thank you so much, Dan. I would be absolutely lost without them. And that was such a brave thing to do."

"It was a great dive," her husband said.

Blushing with pleasure, he turned to the man, who sported the faded red-canvas shorts and white polo shirt favored by the yachting types.

"Thanks. I can do a flip. And a back dive."

"I bet you slapped your back a time or two learning."

"More than that." He grimaced in recollection. "But it's worth it, now." And it was. The hours he had spent learning to dive, mastering his fear, thinking it through, trying and failing and trying again, had given him something that made him different, something he was proud of.

"Are you on the swim team?"

"We don't have one."

"So where'd you learn?" he asked. "Not off this pier?"

Dan shook his head. "Too far a drop. There's a swimming spot upcountry, with a bridge that's close to the water."

The woman took her purse from her shoulder and opened it.

"Here. This is for you."

She held out two twenty-dollar bills. He knew that he should protest, should say, *Oh, there's no need to, really, I'm just glad I could help.* That was what the Lord would want—or at least, that's what his mother would say He'd want: He wants us to be of service to others, to come to their aid without expecting anything in return.

But forty dollars. . . . The new baseball glove he was saving for—there it was, right in her hand, his for the taking.

"Thanks so much, ma'am. That's awesome of you."

That one lucky moment had given him the idea that transformed his teen years, taking him from a kid self-conscious about his cheap secondhand clothes to someone who could wear brand-name jeans and L.L.Bean polo shirts. Who, despite his home circumstances, could now at least blend in with the better-off kids at school. And all because he'd learned to pry money out of the pockets of tourists by betting husbands that he could dive in and retrieve a Kennedy half-dollar from as far out as their wives could throw it from the breakwater.

It had taken some doing to get his routine down right.

At first, he had just approached any prosperous-looking middle-aged man standing with a small mixed group and asked, quietly, if he wanted to make a bet. Mostly what he got in response was a dismissive shake of the head. The few times the conversation went any further was when the man's wife noticed him and asked her husband what he wanted. This taught him that he had to involve the women from the start and, better yet, the entire group. Which meant being a chirpy showman with an element of humorous mystery.

He tried several pitches before arriving at one that was surefire.

"Excuse me, sir," he'd say in a voice loud enough for all four or five or six to hear, "would you like to make an Evel Knievel bet starring your wife?"

Good-humored group curiosity meant he was always asked to explain, and once he did, the answer was almost invariably yes. At first, he'd stipulated that the woman had to throw the coin underhanded, but twice when he had forgotten, they had done so anyway. So he had cut that from his bet terms.

He'd open the slim cherry-stained coin box he'd bought on eBay and let one of the men select a shiny fifty-cent piece from the pair embedded in its crushed velvet nest. Once they chose, you had them. They'd take the coin in their fingers, rub it, toss it gently up and down, sometimes jokingly bite its edge, and then declare it legit and hand it to their wife.

The trick was to time your dive so that you left the pier just after the spinning coin had hit the apex of its trajectory. By then, you could tell where it was going and gauge your dive so that you could spot the splash and see the sunlight glinting on the silver as it slid through the water.

Sometimes after he won the initial bet and was due a ten or a twenty, the men would demand to throw the coin themselves. He'd act dubious at first but then let himself be talked into going double or nothing, as long as they'd agree that the coin's arc had to reach as high as the top of the nearby light pole. They usually said yes without realizing how the physics of such a parabola pushed the odds in his favor.

But some men, intent on winning, would retreat to a starting point halfway back from the bull rail, thereby elongating the initial leg of the toss and angling the half-dollar's downward trajectory farther out into the bay.

When he couldn't retrieve the coin, he'd come back crestfallen.

"Almost," he said. Or "Just missed."

Then he'd open the box, offer up the second half-dollar, and beg for one more chance, at the original terms. Victorious once, most of the men would take a little off their second throw. Not all of them, though. Sometimes that toss would go just as far. He'd slant his dive out and stay under as long as he could, making sure to surface in the vicinity of the splash. Having seen him emerge from the ocean empty-handed once, no one ever suspected that he had a third Kennedy half-dollar rubber-banded into the pocket of his cutoffs, secret insurance against a second defeat.

Those were good memories, and reliving them eased his anger. It was time. He could face it now.

And so, he ambled along Water Street through the North End. Ten minutes later, he stood there at the house that had once seemed like a prison he'd never escape.

CHAPTER 4

THE FRONT DOOR was locked, and he had long ago lost his key. He walked around back, but that door proved unyielding as well.

Now where had she kept it? He let his eyes wander down the stoop and through the scrub grass of the backyard.

The blue gazing ball, there on its chipped stand. Of course.

In the kitchen, the light leaking from the cloudy March sky cast a rectangle on the table, where a half-empty teacup sat next to an open issue of *Ladies' Home Journal.* Wooden tongs lay next to a small plastic plate, and for a moment, he could almost see her leaning over the toaster, lifting a slice of raisin bread and turning it, then dropping it back in to expose the untoasted side to the single heating element that worked.

He walked into the living room and sat down on the rattan love seat. The heat was down, and the room was cold, concentrating the dank odor that drifted up from the dirt cellar on all but the warmest months of the year.

He knew he should be sad. In a way, he wanted the deep ache of loss to overwhelm him, to come in a torrent, to wash away the guilty relief that had crept in at the news.

The call had come early, so early he was still in bed.

"Is Immanuel there?"

He'd almost said no. No one called him that, not even back home. Just his mother when she was mad and never with that plummy accent on the last syllable. He hadn't even thought of the name since he'd been at Bates.

"Who are you trying to reach?"

"Immanuel Winters."

"Who's this?"

"Reverend Abner Peevers, from the Eastport Apostolic Church."

"This is Dan Winters."

"Umm, yes, Dan. I'm sorry to be the bearer of bad news. Your mother has been in an accident. I'm afraid there's no easy way to put this. She has gone to meet the Lord."

He sat up in bed.

"She's dead?"

"Yes."

"What happened?"

"She was driving to Calais to bring one of our congregants home from the hospital. The car went off the road and over the embankment. She was dead by the time the ambulance got there. A broken neck."

"God. What caused it?"

"The police aren't sure. She was driving his car—hers is in the shop—and the tires evidently weren't good. They think she may have hit a patch of black ice. It's been wet the last few days, then it froze yesterday. I'm sorry, Imm—Dan."

He'd thought about stopping by Hannah's dorm to tell her but quickly decided against it. They had been going out just long enough that she might make a dramatic gesture and insist on coming. Better to call when he got there and say that he'd had to leave in a hurry. She had no idea he hadn't seen his mother in more than a year, not since that Thanksgiving when he'd had a four-day furlough from the Center. That she was part of something he'd wanted to seal in the past.

And now he could. She had no people except for her brother down in Texas, where he'd settled after the service. He surely wouldn't come for the funeral. He'd never been any more of a presence than an irregular Christmas card. Too put off by all the religiosity, no doubt.

Or maybe he'd suspected the truth. That had never occurred to him before, and now he rolled the thought over inconclusively.

There was no one else to see, nothing to draw him back ever again. He barely knew the church people who had sustained her all these years. They'd bury her, and he'd head back to college, and then he'd live the life he was making for himself. Just as she'd lived the one she'd made for herself.

Except he'd live like a normal person, and no one would ever know.

CHAPTER 5

"MOM, CAN YOU tell me something I really need to know?"

He had picked his moment, waiting until supper was over, then helping with the dishes, after which she settled in at the kitchen table, needle in hand, humming "A Mighty Fortress Is Our God" as she closed a tear in his Converse high-tops.

"What's that?"

"What was my father like?"

"Ouch. Drat." She eyed her finger, where a bright red drop was forming. "Now see what you made me do." She sucked the tip for a moment and then resumed her sewing.

"Are you gonna tell me?"

"Danny, I've told you before, it's something I don't want to talk about."

"But what am I supposed to say when the other kids ask?"

"Say, MYOB. Besides, you're not the only boy in school with one parent."

"I'm the only one who has never even seen his father and doesn't know a single thing about him."

"Perhaps that's a blessing."

"At least tell me where he is."

"Your Father art in Heaven, hallowed be His name."

"You mean he's dead?"

"I mean the Lord is all the father you need. Trust in Him. He'll provide for you."

He got up from his chair.

"What's He provided for you? This junky little house?"

"Danny, this is your home, and the church is good to let us stay here."

"This is a shithole, and the church is ripping you off. If you worked the same hours somewhere else, even at the IGA, we could rent a better one."

She heaved herself out of her chair, a distraught look darkening her face.

"Immanuel Winters, you go to your room. I don't want to see you again until you're ready to apologize to the Lord. And then to me."

And she'd refused to speak to him until, just before supper the next day, he had gotten on his knees in the kitchen and said a prayer of apology and then told her, too, that he was sorry.

So once again, he had been rebuffed.

If she had just said that he had died in an accident. Or that he had broken things off after she got pregnant and then moved away somewhere. Or even, as he dreaded in those moments when he let himself consider the full range of his fears, that his father was married to someone else.

Anything.

But she wouldn't say a word about him.

His father's absence was the dominant fact of his own life, and her refusal to tell him anything only made the void worse.

CHAPTER 6

HE CLIMBED THE steep stairs and turned left into his old room. It was smaller than he remembered, the eaves lower, the faded blue paper almost white in the wan light from the window. His old baseball glove, the first one he had ever bought, sat atop the composite-board desk, as though tossed there as an afterthought.

He brought it to his nose and inhaled its earthy scent. He had spent hours rubbing neatsfoot oil into the leather to make it soft and supple, then grinding a baseball into the pocket until it was shaped the way he wanted. He loved the smell, the feel, the way it fit his hand, the easy way it came to fold over on itself, the soft *thwap* that rewarded a well-caught ball.

There was something magical about it, something that lingered even now, even though he had one that cost three times as much back at Bates. Convincing his mother to let him buy it had been his first step into the enchanted world of baseball.

And it turned out that baseball had been his ticket out of Eastport, away from its dingy little paint-peeling houses, its downtown of boarded-up brick storefronts, its coves of rotting wharves slowly surrendering to the sea, for baseball more than anything else had gotten Bates to take a chance on him.

He was a solid student—good, even, when the subject engaged him—but Bates could fill its dorms with kids who could do as well or better with less effort. Kids who had read *A Portrait of the Artist as a Young Man* in prep school, who not only understood the basic ebb and flow of the Civil War but even knew which side had won its major battles, who could pronounce Tchaikovsky, and who could immediately identify a painting as one by Marc Chagall or Salvador Dali or Pablo Picasso.

Yet he could do one thing they couldn't. He could take a baseball in his right hand, wind up, and throw it with enough hard spin that it curved down and away and was goddamned hard to hit. Not impossible. He wasn't that good, wasn't good enough for the pros, which meant baseball was a fading ticket. But baseball had gotten him to Bates, baseball and begging, and he was doing well enough there that his diploma would take over when baseball was punched and expired.

Of course, baseball had also led to the fight where he'd half killed Griff Kimball, the fight that had gotten him in such trouble. But a mixed blessing was still a blessing.

Baseball was not the favorite sport in Eastport. Basketball held that honor. There was no football, of course, for it required not just uniforms but all sorts of expensive equipment, from helmets to shoulder pads to kneepads to cleats. A town had to be wealthy or big to afford a team, and most of the places in Downeast Maine were neither.

Every town had a gym, though, and so every high school had a basketball court, and that meant every school had a team. Basketball was popular because games gave the townsfolk somewhere to go and something to chew over during the long Maine winters.

But it was baseball that had caught his imagination. There was something mystical about the idea that you could make a ball curve on its way toward a batter. It was like having a superpower, the way the comic-book heroes did. A superpower more precious because it had taken so long to acquire.

"Did that one curve?"

Benny Bouchard shook his head.

He wound up and threw again.

"How 'bout that one?"

"Nope."

He had been pitching to Benny for half an hour, using a Wiffle ball because it was supposed to be easier to learn with, and he could sense his friend was losing interest. But apparently not enough to offer up an encouraging lie.

"How 'bout that?"

"Uh-uh. Maybe you should just work on your fastball. Or try a spitball?"

"A good pitcher needs a curveball. You try. See if you can do it."

"No. I wanna go swimming. Let's see if your mom'll take us."

Dan looked dubiously at the house.

"She's probably got to go see the old ladies."

"Which ones?"

"The ones she sees on Thursday."

"She sees different ones every day?"

"Yeah."

"Why?"

"For the church."

"Let's check anyways."

"Okay. But if she says no, you gotta catch a few more pitches."

"Maybe."

But he didn't. When Dan's mother said what he knew she'd say, Benny made an excuse, got on his bike, and pedaled back toward his house.

He had checked two books on pitching out of the library, and he studied them every spare moment. Most of it he understood well enough that he at least knew the mechanics he had to practice, the technique he needed to acquire.

But with the curveball, he just couldn't tell. He thought he had the grip right, his middle finger along the stitching on the top of the ball, with his index finger resting lightly beside it, his thumb on the seam on the bottom. Then the windup and the sharp snap of the wrist to release the pitch. It should have been easier with a Wiffle ball, but it wasn't.

He came to think he wouldn't be able to get the pitch to work unless he knew exactly why that snap of the wrist made the baseball curve. That meant going to the library and googling it, and then reading, with painful slowness, through various articles about Bernoulli's principle and the Magnus effect. It didn't make sense at first, but it was the same thing that made planes fly. It had to work, so he kept trying to puzzle it out.

"Dan, would you like to print that article out?" asked Mrs. Clayton, the grandmotherly type who was the small library's sole staffer. "That way you can study it at home."

He hesitated. The sign said the library charged twenty-five cents a page for printing.

"I didn't bring any money."

She smiled.

"It's on me. It'll be my investment in the future of the baseball team."

Even with the article's diagram, it was hard slogging. If the ball was thrown with enough snap, the spin would increase the speed of the airflow on the side of ball that rotated back toward the pitcher.

But why not on both sides?

He read and stared and sat and thought and read again before it came to him.

The key was to think of the other air—the air the ball was moving through. Because the ball was going forward, the air meeting the ball would be like a wind blowing against it, and the air spurred into motion by the spin of the ball would be colliding with that wind for the first half of the rotation.

But not for the second half. Once beyond the midpoint, the air current created by the spin would be going in the same direction as the wind. That meant the combined currents would move faster. More speed meant less pressure, and less pressure meant the ball would tail in that direction, because there would be more pressure on other side.

Now that he had it in his head, he had to make sure the knowledge wouldn't slip away, as things learned in school so often did. He replicated the diagram on notebook paper and added his own labeled arrows showing the different airflows and the resulting changes in pressure, and he reviewed the article and diagram each night. Then he'd lie there in the dark, refusing to let himself drift off to sleep until he could picture it happening, step by step.

And then he'd practice it each afternoon, throwing at an old tire he'd covered with a piece of musty canvas and hung on the side of their ramshackle shed.

The other great thing about baseball was that it was free. It was the one American sport you could follow in northeastern Maine even if you didn't have a television. TV was a worldly corruption they didn't need, his mother said, something that slipped the tawdry underside of American culture in under God's guard.

But a radio was something anyone could afford, and the Red Sox were always on the radio. It was an almost unbelievable gift: a full schedule of games you could hear just by turning it on—games where every moment would be brought to life, every decision analyzed, where the sudden excitement of a well-hit ball could be traced in the rising pitch of the announcer's voice.

Just by listening, you could learn the ploys and strategies and statistics, and he had taken an outsized pride in his growing knowledge of the game. Even if you hadn't watched the TV shows other kids talked about, knowing about baseball gave you something to say, something that helped disguise the big gaps that separated your world from theirs.

And so, baseball became a secret oasis there in the desert of his childhood. At night, he would lie on his bed with the volume down low, close his eyes, and pretend he was there in Fenway Park—that his father had taken him and they were part of the excited crowd when a loud cheer rose after the crack of bat on ball.

Occasionally he would fall asleep while he listened, and the daydream would become a real dream. When it did, his father would assume the dulcet narrative of the play-by-play man, describing the game as it took place before them.

Yet when he would turn from the field to look over at him, his face would be lost in the shadow of the Red Sox cap he wore, the only discernible feature a pair of moving lips.

CHAPTER 7

HE FOUND HIMSELF studying other boys and their fathers. Some men were so lost in their own thoughts that they only seemed to remember they had kids when a son or daughter would put a question to them.

"Hmm?" David Doherty's dad would invariably ask. "What's that again, champ?"

He was the same way at Little League games.

"Remember to congratulate him on his hits," he overheard Mrs. Doherty say as the couple waited for David after a game.

"How many did he get?"

"Three."

"And what were they?"

"Hmm . . . I would have sworn that man sitting next to me was you, but I guess not."

Mr. Doherty had laughed ruefully.

"Sorry, sweetheart. Thinking about work, I guess."

Other fathers had nothing but the game on their mind—and had expectations so high that their sons lived in constant fear of falling short.

"Jesus Christ, Jimmy, never swing on three and oh," he heard one father yell after his son had taken an awkward cut at a low pitch. Watching the boy then stand numbly as two called strikes whizzed by, he could almost feel his humiliation.

And yet, he often saw the same man at the diamond in early evening, hitting pop flies for his son to catch or grounders for him to run down. So maybe with fathers like that, you just had to take the bad with the good.

And then there were the fathers whose perpetual annoyance always seemed about to erupt into an angry outburst.

In the late summer after freshman year, he'd been trolling the breakwater, looking for tourists to dive for. It was a rare Maine day without a cloud in the sky, the bay a sparkling, ever-changing mosaic of rippling blues created by wind and current. The tide was still a little too high to make the leap long enough to spur a bet, so he had wandered the inner perimeter, gazing down at the boats tied there.

"You weren't even close to the goddamn thing."

A wiry teenager about his own height stood on the work dock in his underwear, hair wet, shivering under a towel.

"It's just so freaking cold."

"Don't be such a goddamn sissy. Just get the hell down there, and run the rope through the damn handle. It won't take more than a couple of seconds."

As he walked down the cleated gangway, Dan could see the boy peering into the water. He dropped the towel and, taking a rope in his hand, dove again. He stayed down for longer than Dan expected, but when he broke the surface, failure was written on his face.

"I can't get down that far."

"You're looking to me for hundreds of bucks to get your damn tooth fixed, and you can't even get this done? If my father had needed me to do it when I was your age, I wouldn't have given up if it'd taken me all day."

"If you think it's so easy, why don't you try?"

"You watch your goddamn mouth."

"What's down there?"

The man turned Dan's way and looked at him through hooded eyes. His pouched face and balding bullet head had the habitually sunburned look of someone who worked the water.

"Mind your own business."

"Maybe I could get it."

"What makes you think you could when he couldn't?"

Dan glanced at the man's son, who stared balefully and then

mouthed what looked like "asshole" at him.

"I do some diving off the breakwater, so I'm used to the cold. It's fierce."

"You the kid who's always showing off for the tourists?"

"Just trying to earn some money."

"Yeah, well, my toolbox is down there. It's worth ten bucks if you can get a rope through the handle."

Peering over the edge of the dock, Dan could see the red metal box resting on the bottom in water that looked to be about twenty feet deep.

"That's a long way down. How about twenty?"

"When I was your age, I'd have done it for free."

"It hurts my ears something wicked, going that deep. My head aches all day."

"But twenty would make the pain bearable?"

"Yeah."

"You're a regular Shylock, kid."

What did that mean? Dan answered with a palms-up shrug.

Scowling, the man appraised him for a moment.

"I'll go fifteen."

"Okay."

"So here's what I need you to do: Run this rope through the handle, then bring it back up."

Dan knelt and arranged the rope in loose coils that would play out without snagging. When that was done, he stripped to his swimsuit and dove. The still water on the breakwater's lee side was a little less frigid than he had expected, but bottom was a long way down. Ten hard strokes and he still wasn't there. His breath was starting to grow short. Five more. Four more. Three more. He could do it.

Two more. Now the toolbox was in front of him. Grabbing the handle, he pulled himself to it and reeved the rope through, then pushed hard off the rocky bottom. Two seconds later, he broke the surface, gasped some air, and held up the taped end.

The man took it and turned to his son.

"See how easy it was? Now, you think you could hold this end and not let go while I pull the goddamn thing up?"

"Why not just tie it to the cleat?"

"Why not just do what I said?"

With that, he handed the wet end of the rope to the kid and knelt and pulled hand over hand on the other side of the line.

Seeing the teen bracing hard against the weight, Dan stepped over to help. As he did, the kid swung an elbow that just missed his shoulder.

The red toolbox came steadily nearer and then broke the surface.

The man grabbed the handle and pulled it up onto the dock. Water trickled from the hinge. He opened the box and started removing the tools. When they were arrayed on the floating dock, he went to his boat and returned with a ratty towel and a can of WD-40 and started wiping them down with oil.

"Can I get my money?"

The man riffled through his grungy cloth wallet, pulled out two fives, and extended them toward Dan.

"We said fifteen."

"And now I'm saying that all you're gettin' is ten. You weren't in the water for more than thirty seconds."

"Seems to me if you promised him fifteen, you owe him fifteen."

He turned to see Jonah Grady, the harbormaster, about halfway down the gangway. The first man eyed the new arrival, who wore a bill cap over short gray hair, as he walked the rest of the way down to the floating dock.

"How's this any of your business?"

"Well, what happens on the breakwater concerns the harbormaster, and it says here that I'm the harbormaster," Grady said, pointing to a patch above the right pocket of his denim work shirt. "And unless I'm mistaken, you're the fella who wanted to see me about something."

"Yeah. Some SOB hard-waked me and knocked my tools in the water."

"Before we get into that, you prob'ly want to finish your business dealings," the harbormaster said.

"What's the going price here for thirty seconds of salvage work?"

"I'd say getting your toolbox back right when you need it is worth at least fifteen bucks. Maybe even twenty."

Extracting another five from his wallet, the man crumpled the three bills in his fist and dropped them on the dock. Dan scrambled to scoop the money up before the light breeze carried it into the water. He forced a "thank you" he didn't feel and then turned toward gangway, where Grady stood with a frown wrinkling his forehead.

"You all set?"

Dan nodded.

"Okay, then," the harbormaster said, shifting his gaze to the man, "why don't we start over? I'm Jonah Grady, the harbormaster. And you're . . . ?"

"Curt Beal."

"And what can I do you for, Curt?"

"Some son of a bitch in a boat named the *Betty Anne* circled way back here and then roared off like a bat out of hell. His wake pretty near had me swimming. I had to drop my toolbox to keep from going in."

"Well, now, I know the captain of the *Betty Anne*, and that don't sound like him. He's about as nice a fella as could be, so long as you stay on the right side of him."

"What's that supposed to mean?"

"What it means is you haven't been around here long, Curt. Moved up from Jonesport this year, isn't that right?"

Beal spat in the water and then brought both hands to his hips.

"So me being from away makes it okay to hard-wake my boat?"

"No, 'course it don't." Grady took his sunglasses out of his shirt pocket and spent a second or two cleaning them on the front of his shirt. "Still, folks will do it when they want to send a message."

"What kind of message?"

"With lobstermen, there are only ever two kinds of messages. Your traps are too close on mine, or my traps are coming up light."

"I'm not close on anybody."

"Must be the other, then."

"My traps are coming up light, too."

Grady half turned and looked across the rows of boats.

"The thing is the local guys don't know that. You sell over to Lubec, right?"

"Yeah."

"Why's that?"

"The guy there's a friend of mine."

"Walter Pike, you mean?"

"Yeah. Walter Pike."

"Known him long?"

Beal looked guardedly at him.

"Long enough to do business with."

"Well, then, you must know him as Waddy, which is what he's mostly called. Provided we're talking the same fella."

"What're you getting at?"

Grady took his cap off, ran his right hand through his hair, and then pulled it back onto his head.

"That when most everybody is selling to Stimley's, you can see how they'd start to wonder why the new boat's going all the way over to Lubec."

"I just said. He's a friend of mine."

"Waddy."

"Yeah, Waddy."

"The other thing is you're out awful early."

"No law against that. Not yet anyway."

"No, but it sets people to wondering."

"Let 'em wonder. But if anyone wants to accuse me of pulling their traps, they'd damn well better be ready to prove it in court."

The harbormaster frowned.

"The fishermen down to Jonesport may be courthouse types, but that's generally not the way things get done up here. Folks send a message, and if it don't register, they send another—usually louder, so to speak. Which is why I always hope a word to the wise does the trick. God knows, things are rough enough out on the water without mixing in bad blood."

He eyed Beal for a moment, then spoke again.

"And now, Curt, I'll track down the captain of the *Betty Anne* and tell him that you and I had a talk. And I'll remind him that the lee side of the breakwater is a no-wake zone."

Dan had been standing off to the side, taking in the exchange.

Now that it was over, he started up the sloping gangway. Glancing back, he saw the other kid glaring at him. He still hadn't broken his stare when, reaching the top of the breakwater, Dan looked back one last time.

CHAPTER 8

THE GNAWING NEED to find out about his own father had spurred him to scour the house for something, anything, that might shed some light on the mystery.

One Saturday midway through his junior year, a Saturday when his mother had gone with her church group to deliver Christmas cookies to shut-ins, he had begun his search.

In a house as small as theirs, there weren't many places to look. One lower cabinet in the kitchen held a box of old bills, bank statements, and curled-up receipts, but though he went through the entire stash, he could find nothing interesting.

Upstairs, under the eaves, there were only the two bedrooms. Hers contained little but a bed, a nightstand with several shelves, and a pine dresser that partially blocked the room's single window. There were a few boxes under the bed, one full of *Good Housekeeping* magazines, another bulging with rayon sweaters and assorted extra pairs of the thick gray socks she padded around the house in during winter, the last stuffed with Sunday-service bulletins copied on cheap gray paper and old hymnals.

Which left only the dresser.

His determination tinctured with a brief wash of shame, he poked through drawers full of beige undergarments, cotton blouses, and stretch pants.

But there was nothing there, either.

All that remained was the attic crawlspace.

He went out back to the shed and retrieved the weather-beaten stepladder. Standing on it, he pushed up the painted plywood cover and set it to one side, then climbed into the dark space. It was damp and smelled of mildew but too dark to see a thing.

He went back for the only flashlight he could find, a penlight that cast an abbreviated crescent on the rough underside of the roofing boards.

Two boxes sat within easy reach, obviously put there by someone standing on the ladder. The first held some bright summer dresses and a purple paisley blouse, things his mother must have grown too heavy for even before his earliest adolescent recollection, since they conjured up not even the faintest simulacrum of memory.

The second had things of his. Some baby shoes, a toddler's pair of overalls, and the white stuffed dog he'd slept with as a boy. *Brannew*, he had called it, a shortening of "Brand-New Doggy." Having seen him through childhood, it was now patched and stained and looked thoroughly forlorn. He stuffed the old rag dog back in the box, then pulled it out again and tossed it down into the hall.

The box pushed against something as he slid it back in place.

He reached a hand behind it and brought out a small metal case. It was secured by a cheap built-in lock.

He carried it and the stuffed dog to his room, then went to the kitchen and rooted around for a paper clip or bobby pin. In the detective novels he read, locks were always being picked with those implements, surrendering with a sudden click to deft ministrations. However, ten minutes of fiddling brought no such noise nor even the feel of motion.

Where would his mother keep the key?

He carried the box back to her room, set it on the bed, and, on a hunch, lifted the thick black Bible from the shelf of the nightstand. He'd wondered idly before why she kept two Bibles in the room, the small white one within easy reach next to the lamp, the large black one below.

Opening it, he thumbed through the onionskin leaves. They parted naturally at the first page of Matthew, and there, he saw the small silver key.

As he picked it up, his eyes caught the verse imprinted with its shape: "Behold, a virgin shall be with child and shall bring forth a son and they shall call his name Immanuel; which being interpreted is, God with us."

Now the lock turned and clicked, and he pushed the side buttons and lifted the cover. The case held one thick manila envelope, fastened with a thin string that wrapped around a cardboard disk.

He carefully unwound the string, lifted the thin cardboard flap, and took out the paper.

He expected some sort of embossed seal, some official stamp of authenticity, as a birth certificate might carry. But it was just ordinary white paper, one page, folded in thirds the way he had been taught to crease a business letter for mailing.

Unfolding the page, he could see it was a Xerox copy. Centered at the top of the page was a simple heading LUBEC POLICE DEPARTMENT CRIMINAL INCIDENT REPORT. Down an inch, above a series of widely spaced lines, were instructions to PLEASE PRINT and DESCRIBE THE INCIDENT IN AS MUCH DETAIL AS YOU CAN REMEMBER.

Printed in a girlish hand on the lines below, he read:

My name is Clara Winters. Shortly after midnight on the night of July 3, I was walking home from the dance at Lubec High School. I was late, so I took a shortcut along the railroad tracks. As I was walking along the bank where it drops away near the ocean, a guy I had seen at the dance came out of the trees on the other side and grabbed me and pulled me behind the bushes. I started to scream, but he held his hand over my mouth and put a knife against my neck and said if I did it again, he'd "gut me like a fish and throw me in the ocean." He pushed me down and got on top of me. Then he pulled my dress up and ripped my underwear off and raped me. When he was done, he said I was a "cock-teasing" C-word "who got what she deserved." He said I had to wait half an hour before I left the spot and that he'd be watching and that if I didn't wait, he'd catch me and kill me. Then he left. I waited for a while, then I ran home.

CHAPTER 9

HE SAT STARING at the paper until the words blurred, hoping that as the print lost shape, its meaning, too, would fade.

He thought of his own birthday, April 5, silently counted the months, though there was no need. He knew they'd match.

Blood of my blood, flesh of my flesh. Father, son.

Unholy ghost.

He tried to imagine his mother, in a younger version, walking along the darkened path, the figure lying in wait, tense, crouched, judging the moment to spring, his mother shouting, a rough hand closing over her mouth, muffling her cry.

His mind rebelled.

His mother. Why her, with her sad, distant eyes, her dull, home-cut hair, her chunky figure, heavy hips?

Maybe she hadn't always looked that way. Perhaps back then she had been pretty and lively, with cheeks that dimpled when she smiled, eyes that sparkled under her bangs, smooth legs pleasing in their muscled taper, a girl worth watching, worth stalking, worth lying in wait for . . .

"Uhhh." The sound burst involuntarily from him. He was thinking like the man who had raped his mother. Thinking like his father. The shock of that realization struck him so palpably it left a wave of nausea.

Suddenly, he recalled a conversation on the back of the team bus, on the ride home from Woodland. If you knew you could get away with it and that no one would ever know, someone had asked, which of the high-school cheerleaders would you trap in a dark room and force yourself on?

Casually, analytically, they had discussed each guy's choice. Maria Marlson, with her hour-glass figure and dark mane of loose curls.

Bonnie Rogers, with her lush lips, melodic laugh, and breasts that bounced so captivatingly in her V-neck gym shirt. Alyson Dolph, whose angular cheekbones, long legs, and sculpted butt gave her the exotic appearance of a runway model. Karen Wheatley, with her cute button nose and twin-dimpled girl-next-door innocence.

No one had objected, no one had said, *Wait—how can we even talk this way?* Not even when Julian Rush, the second to choose Alyson, had offered his own dark reason.

"I hate that bitch." he'd said. "She thinks she's so goddamn gorgeous and smart, she's such a fucking snob. By the time I got done, she'd cry so hard her makeup would look like the Joker. And then I'd jizz all over her tits."

And no one had said a word, no one except Paul Parker, who had been the first to pick Alyson.

"I guess I'd better go first, then, because otherwise it sounds like I'd be getting pretty sloppy seconds."

And they had all howled, reduced to such hysterics that Mr. Healey had wandered back from his seat behind the driver to ask what was so funny, seemingly miffed when, still gasping and wiping their eyes, they had waved him away.

CHAPTER 10

WHENCE COME WE? What are we? Whither go we?

When they had studied Gauguin's famous painting in art class, he had felt little beyond a vague interest in the half-naked females in the exotic scene. But now similar questions burned in him. Like the painter, he sometimes seemed to himself wild, untamed. Or going feral because of something beyond his control.

Reading *Hamlet* for English class, he labored, belatedly and bored, through prose that seemed more code than English, until he fell upon the words Hamlet speaks while waiting for his father's ghost to reappear.

There it was again, the same haunting idea, this time in the form of a "vicious mole" in the nature of a man, a passed-down trait he is blameless for "since nature cannot chose his origin," but which still imparts "the stamp of one defect" that outweighs countless virtues to shape his fate.

Suddenly, everyday comments and conversation seemed full of assertions about paternity's claims. A chip off the old block. Like father, like son. The apple doesn't fall far from the tree. What's bred in the bone comes through in the flesh.

He'd heard those chestnuts countless times, always spoken as accepted truths. More often still, he'd heard old people assigning traits of progeny to the influence of forebears.

So, the mischievous sparkle in David Doherty's eyes was said to come from his mother, who "had the very devil in her" as a girl, just as Ronnie Young was told "you get your foolishness from your father" when he played the clown, and Bret Dunbarton was assured that he "burned the same coal as used to warm your grandfather" when his temper raged.

But nobody ever said anything like that to him. Of course, they hadn't known his mother in her girlhood. Still, in a town where it seemed that every young person was assured on a weekly basis that he or she was "the spitting image" of a mother or father, grandmother or grandfather, he didn't resemble his mother at all. She had light brown hair, a rosy complexion, and full lips. And she verged on the sloppy obesity he associated with poverty and shabbiness.

He himself, however, was darker and more angular, with skin that tanned fast even in the mild sun of a Downeast spring and stretched as tight under his chin as a cat's vellum. His wiry walnut hair had none of his mother's curls, and his dark brows traced thin vivid lines across his forehead.

Her nose, which separated warm blue eyes, turned up at the end, his broke downward in a shape he had learned was aquiline, and his eyes were a deep gray above sharp, slanted cheeks.

No, no one ever said he was his mother's son.

"Cassius looks like Dan," someone had cracked when they had read *Julius Caesar* aloud in class. Listening to the description of the assassin's lean and hungry appearance, he had been thinking the same thing.

Had his father looked that way as well?

CHAPTER 11

HIS QUESTIONS HAD sent him sorting through old newspapers, for the knowledge had triggered a cancerous curiosity. He first tried the local library, which kept years of back issues of the *Quoddy Tides*, the folksy, Eastport-based biweekly that served the area, but in its pages, he found nothing.

And so, one unseasonably mild Saturday shortly after the turn of the year, he hitchhiked the fifty miles to Machias to use the library at the Downeast branch of the University of Maine. It had the *Bangor Daily News* on microfilm, which he threaded between the twin glass plates of the viewing machine, focusing the lens before spooling his way slowly through the issues from that summer.

In early August of that year, he had found a short report. Under the headline HOLDEN MILLS MAN CHARGED, it read:

> A Washington County grand jury yesterday indicted Lester A. Fortin, 25, of Holden Mills, on charges of rape in connection with a July 3 incident in Lubec. Fortin, a Navy sailor, came to Lubec aboard the USS *Saturn*, which the Navy sent to participate in the Fourth of July celebration. Fortin's arrest came after a 17-year-old Lubec girl reported being attacked and raped while walking home from a July 3 dance. Fortin is being held on $20,000 bail.

Several weeks later, there had been another brief mention: Fortin had been formally arraigned, had pled not guilty, and was being represented by a Navy lawyer.

It took him an hour before he found another story, under the headline NAVY MAN CLAIMS ENCOUNTER WAS CONSENSUAL. Again, the account was without a photograph, even though it marked the start of the trial.

> A Navy sailor charged with rape as the result of an alleged July 3 attack in Lubec yesterday told a Washington County Superior Court that he had had sex with the 17-year-old girl in question but insisted their encounter was consensual.
>
> Defendant Lester Fortin, 25, of Holden Mills, who took the stand yesterday in a Machias courtroom, said that he had met the alleged victim at the dance, that the two had spent much of the evening together, and that the girl had asked him to walk her home when it came time for her to leave. They stopped in a secluded spot along the way and had sexual relations, he said, adding that they had parted amicably.
>
> "I was shocked when the police pulled me off the ship a month or so later," said Fortin, an enlisted man with the rank of petty officer third class. His ship, the USS *Saturn*, was in Lubec for several days this summer as part of the Fourth of July celebration.
>
> Fortin's account sharply contradicted that of the Lubec girl. Before he took the stand, she told the court that Fortin had suddenly appeared from behind a stand of small trees as she walked along a remote path.
>
> "He said, 'Hi again, it's just me,'" she told the court in a faltering voice. "He said he just wanted to walk with me, but all of a sudden, he clamped his hand over my mouth. Then he put a knife to my throat and said if I screamed, he'd kill me."
>
> The girl, whose name is being withheld in accordance with *Bangor Daily News* policy pertaining to possible victims of sexual assault, said she had danced with Fortin "two or three times" at the July 3 dance

at Lubec High School and conceded they had kissed briefly during a slow dance but insisted that was the extent of their physical involvement.

"He was trying to make out, but I just wanted to dance," she said.

However, Nathan Moats, a fellow sailor from the USS *Saturn* and a self-described friend of Fortin, said he had been on the dance floor at the time and had noticed that the two were getting what he described as "pretty physical."

"It was like, get a room!" he said. "She seemed really into him."

The high-school student said she left the dance by herself at about midnight because she had to be home by 12:30, while her friends had permission to stay until the event ended.

In his testimony, however, Fortin said the two had not only danced together repeatedly but, at one point, had left the auditorium to drink Southern Comfort outside.

"We were drinking and making out behind the school," he said. "And she was letting me put my hands pretty much anywhere I wanted, so when she asked me to walk her home, I knew we were thinking the same thing." He said the girl had gone alone to say good-bye to her friends but had asked him to rejoin her outside, so people wouldn't see them leaving together.

"I guess she didn't want a lot of gossip," he said.

Under cross-examination from Captain James Davies, the Navy attorney representing Fortin, the girl acknowledged she had drunk some wine with her friends before the dance but said she was not intoxicated. She also denied leaving the dance to drink with Fortin and said the one time she had gone outside, it had been by herself.

"I just went out for a cigarette," she insisted.

When Davies asked how she could have been raped without bruising or other marking of some sort—the prosecution has acknowledged there was no evidence of physical injury—the girl said that after Fortin had pulled out a knife, she had ceased any attempts to struggle because she feared for her life.

During his questioning of Moats, Fortin's fellow sailor and friend, Davies asked if he had ever known Fortin to carry a knife or, indeed, even seen him with one.

"I mean, maybe on KP, but not other than that," he said, using the military term for Kitchen Patrol.

Two Lubec police officers who had searched the scene of the alleged rape said they had not found a knife. A Navy investigator who had gone through Fortin's personal gear after his arrest also acknowledged she had not found a knife.

Davies also called to the stand Dr. Elise Crane, a physician at Down East Community Hospital in Machias, who treated the girl the morning after the rape. Under Davies' pointed questioning, she said she hadn't noticed any marks on the girl's neck that would have indicated a sharp object had been pressed against it.

"But honestly, I didn't look that closely," Crane said. "She seemed very upset, and I didn't doubt that it had happened."

Under questioning from Assistant District Attorney Polly Phillips, Lubec High School English instructor Agnes Brizbee, one of the dance chaperones, said she recalled the young woman leaving the dance briefly sometime after 10:00 p.m.

Although Brizbee said she also recalled a sailor leaving at about the same time, the teacher told the court she couldn't say whether it was Fortin. She witnessed no conversation or interaction that would have indicated the two were together, she said.

The girl reentered the dance after twenty minutes or so by herself, Brizbee said, adding that she hadn't noticed if the sailor had also returned at that time.

"I know all the high-school kids by sight, but the sailors all kind of look the same to me," she said.

Brizbee testified that she had no reason to think the young woman was under the influence of alcohol when she returned but admitted she couldn't be sure.

"Kids get high-spirited at dances," she said. "Sometimes it's kind of hard to tell."

The chaperone said she couldn't say for certain when the girl had left the dance for the final time. "They are in and out of the door all night," she said.

Before Fortin first took the stand, his lawyer questioned his commanding officer, Captain Samuel Sanborn, who read several commendations for Fortin made by his superiors. Describing Fortin as "quiet and reserved to the point of being shy," Sanborn stressed that the sailor was diligent about his duties.

"He has always been one of the most responsible men under my command," the captain said. "I just can't believe he'd do this."

Four days later, another story indicated that the jury seemed to have reached an impasse but that the judge had sternly adjured them to listen to one another's arguments and do their best to arrive at a conclusion.

He knew by now he wouldn't find a picture, but he had become fascinated by the accounts of the trial. He thumbed through two more papers before he found the next story, SAILOR GUILTY IN RAPE OF LUBEC TEEN.

Most of the jurors had declined to speak to the press, so the story said little about how the jury had moved beyond deadlock to reach a verdict.

"It was a very tough decision because of the lack of physical evidence," one juror told the paper. "But she seemed like a good, God-fearing Maine girl, and he was a sailor eight years older than her."

The story jumped further inside, and he followed it to the last column of type, which said that Fortin, in his Navy dress whites, had stood according to the judge's instructions before the jury foreman spoke but had slumped to his seat upon hearing the word "guilty."

"It's a lie, and now you've ruined my life," he had said, his voice, in the judgment of the reporter, "filling the courtroom with echoes of the anguish reflected on his face."

Fortin hadn't been sentenced on the day the verdict came in, and the *Bangor Daily News* account didn't specify a date on which the judge had handed down his prison term, so he kept scrolling in search of that story.

He found the sentencing story three weeks further on, paired with a piece headlined RAPE VERDICT, SENTENCE, DIVIDE DOWNEAST TOWN:

> Residents of Lubec, Maine, a small lobstering and fishing village about thirty miles northeast of Machias, reacted in sharply different ways to the guilty verdict a jury handed down in the rape trial of a Navy sailor, and the nine-year sentence Judge Alton Clarke imposed yesterday only heightened the divisions.
>
> Last month, Fortin, 25, of Holden Mills, Maine, was found guilty of raping a 17-year-old Lubec high-school student, whose name is being withheld in accordance with *Bangor Daily News* policy pertaining to victims of sexual assault. The attack took place while the victim was walking home after having left a July 3

dance. Some residents had questioned the jury's guilty verdict, and the sentence Fortin received has left others feeling that the punishment was simply too harsh.

"There just wasn't any evidence of force, and they never found the knife she said he had," said Dolly Swanton, 73, a lifelong Lubec resident who said she attended several days of the trial proceedings.

"I don't know if he did it or not," said Neville Norton, a Lubec lobsterman who said he had read all the coverage of the trial. "I do know that sometimes a girl gets a guy all revved up and then slams on the brakes, and it can be hard for him to stop. So it seems to me probation or a couple of months in jail would be a lot more fair than nine years, especially since it was just her word against his."

But others, while agreeing the sentence seemed long, said they did not believe the 17-year-old would fabricate such an account. Her classmates described the victim as a good student who, though quiet in class, was considered friendly and funny by those who knew her best.

"Some of the guys around town are trying to make it seem like she's all wild and everything, and she's really not," said one female classmate who asked not to be identified. "I mean, it's not like she's a prude, but she's not, like, a party girl either."

Still, a male high-school senior noted that the young woman had acknowledged during Fortin's trial that she had danced with him several times at the event and engaged in a kiss with him during a slow dance.

"Like, if she was making out with the guy, who really knows what happened?" he said.

The victim had left the dance about midnight and was walking home. She told the court that Fortin had suddenly come from behind her as she walked, had held a knife to her throat, and had threatened to kill her if she cried out. Fortin, however, insisted to the court that he had been walking with her, that he had not had a weapon, and that their encounter had been consensual.

Exacerbating the tension is the fact that two of the sailors on Fortin's ship, the USS *Saturn*, grew up in Lubec. Indeed, that's one of the reasons the Navy selected the corvette, the smallest class of Navy ship, to go to Lubec to participate in its Fourth of July celebration. Several of those interviewed by the *Bangor Daily News* said they had heard from those two that Fortin was generally well regarded on board.

In a phone interview from Naval Station Norfolk, Virginia, one of Fortin's Lubec-raised shipmates said that in his experience, Fortin got along with everyone.

"He may not be the life of the party, but he's somebody you like once you get to know him," said Kyle Wyman, who added that Fortin had told him how much he'd enjoyed visiting Lubec for the holiday.

Several people interviewed in Lubec's small downtown said that prior to the USS *Saturn*, it had been years since the town had had a Navy ship in attendance over the Fourth of July. They worried that the *Saturn* might be the last for a while.

"I can't imagine they'll want to come back after all this hullabaloo," said Jerry Vaxton, a lobsterman having coffee at a local diner.

CHAPTER 12

NONE OF THE stories had included a photograph of Fortin, not even one of those mug shots that invariably leaves the just-arrested looking like an aspiring ax murderer or an escapee from a psych ward.

Still, Dan came to realize that he did have a picture in his mind, just as when he read a short story or a book, he developed mental pictures of the characters. But that was because the basic appearances, tall or short, slim or heavy, dark locks or light, well dressed or slovenly, were usually sketched in words by the author. Not so here. None of the stories had even described him. And yet in his mind's eye, he was wiry, about six feet, with dark eyes—almost piercing eyes, really—set in a lean face of taut skin, above a sharp, angular nose.

But where had he gotten that notion?

And then it came to him. He had created Fortin in his own image.

Did they look the same?

Christ, he hoped not. That would bring it all closer, stamp it indelibly on him.

Where would there be a photo? A high-school yearbook was the obvious place.

He called the high school in Holden Mills, but they only had a part-time librarian, and when he finally reached her, she offered little help.

"You could come here during school hours and look through the old yearbooks, as long as it's okay with Central Office," she said, "but there's no way I can send it to you."

He was more than two hundred miles away and without a car, he said. Could she possibly copy the page featuring one of that year's seniors and send it to him?

"I'm sorry. If I were a full-time librarian and had an assistant, the way they do in Bangor, maybe I could," she said. "But it's just me, trying to keep our books in order while working three half-days a week. I wish I had world enough and time, but I just don't."

It was Mrs. Clayton, Eastport's librarian, who came up with an idea that turned out to be successful: They would contact the Holden Mills public library, inquire as to whether they had a collection of yearbooks, and if so, ask to have that one sent as part of the Maine's interlibrary loan program.

He filled out the form, and through the strange call-and-response scream of the library's antique fax machine, they set the request on its way.

He waited a week before he even let himself think about asking and then held off for three days more.

"Not yet, Dan. They don't pay for fast delivery on requests like this."

He checked midweek for each of the next two weeks, then left it for a week and stopped back in the following Monday. Still nothing.

But that Friday, when he was sitting in study hall, Mrs. Randall called him up to where she sat at the front of the large room.

"Mrs. Clayton called from the library. She's got something there for you."

"You've got it for two months, Dan," the librarian said when she handed him the package. "I'm required by the rules of the program to urge you to take good care of it and not to read it while you are eating or drinking, so nothing gets spilled on it. But I'm sure I don't need to tell you that."

"I'll be careful."

He hadn't opened the padded mailing envelope until he was home in his room.

The yearbook had a blue cover with an inlay of gold spelling "Holden Mills High" and the year.

He opened it, and an assortment of faces stared up at him from a different era. Girls with hair that was usually long and parted on the side in a casual, come-as-you-are style, but still occasionally moussed and pulled into a tangled puff above their heads, guys with carefully curated tousled looks.

He turned the pages slowly, fascinated by the faces, the quotes, the sayings, the ambitions.

"Just a dream and the wind to carry me, and soon I'll be free," read the inscription beneath a smiling blonde whose ambition was "to become a flight attendant and travel the world."

"Baby, we were born to run," declared a curly-haired boy, who listed his motorcycle as the place his heart lay.

"What a long, strange trip it's been," seemed an apt summation for a blank-faced teen who listed nothing for activities.

"Two hearts that beat as one, our lives have just begun," captured the sentiments of a doe-eyed Cindi, whose ambition was "to marry Greg and live on a horse farm," while Rodney, with a mop of curls and a mischievous smile, boasted that "love's been a little bit hard on me."

Three more turned pages, and there was Lester Fortin.

The closely cropped hair stood out amid the male dishevelment-by-design of the time. In this photo, at least, he didn't appear intense or on edge or troubled, just bored.

The eyes—did they look like his? Some, Dan thought. His hair was cut too close to tell if there was any resemblance there. A half-smirk had sneaked onto his countenance, suggested mostly by the asymmetrical curl of his lips at the left side of his mouth. That was a look he frequently felt on his own face, but what teenager didn't include it in his expressive repertoire?

Nor, in a straight-on photo, could he tell if their noses seemed similar.

"He'll either find a way or he'll make one" was the phrase that supposedly summed him up. His downfall was "45 mph in a 25-mph zone," his favorite pastime, hunting. "Damn straight" was his favorite saying, "To join the Navy and rule the waves" his avowed ambition. His heart lay "anywhere but here."

In the last will and testament section, where seniors left supposed quirks or quiddities to underclassmen, his was a short and simple sentiment.

"I, Lester Fortin, just leave."

He kept the yearbook a week, opening it at random times and in various lights to look for a greater resemblance.

On Saturday, he went to the barber and asked for a high-and-tight cut.

When he returned, his mother had left on one of her church errands. He took the yearbook to the bathroom, which had the only mirror in the house, held its opened pages next to his face, and practiced the same slight smirk.

Now the dual images in the medicine-cabinet mirror looked almost like twins. So it was an inner inclination that really controlled the resemblance.

The following Saturday, he returned the yearbook to Mrs. Clayton, but not before making several copies of the page that included Fortin's photograph.

CHAPTER 13

THE KNOWLEDGE OF his paternity was made heavier still by the way it hung in his consciousness like a thunderhead in middle distance—neither close enough to threaten immediate danger nor remote enough to lapse beyond regular worry.

In that way, it mirrored the relationship between Eastport and Lubec, two towns that, on fogless days, lived within each other's distant gaze but were otherwise so remote that they might have existed in different times.

You could thank the deep recesses of the Maine coastline for that. By water, Lubec was less than three miles away, but step into a car, and all that changed. A motorist had to travel miles to the west and south to make his way around the broad reaches and long fingers of all the various bays. First, you had to skirt Cobscook, then Dennys, then Whiting, and finally South.

By the time you arrived in Lubec, you'd traveled five-sixths of a circle, motoring almost forty miles on secondary roads to reach a town whose houses and steeples could be seen from the Eastport breakwater.

And when you got there, what you found was pretty much what you'd left: a dwindling, down-on-its-luck town trying to reinvent itself as artsy and quaint for tourists but absent the businesses and services a thriving area needs.

No wonder, then, that most Eastporters, if they had visited Lubec at all, had done so only once or twice. Even then, it was usually just as a stop on a trip to take a vacationing friend or relative to Canada's Campobello Island to see President Franklin Delano Roosevelt's summer place, which loomed palatially across the water from Eastport but was only accessible via the international bridge in Lubec.

There was little social interchange between the two coastal communities. No one he knew had relatives there. His mother no longer did. Once her parents' teenage marriage had broken up, both had left, him to join a New Bedford–based fishing crew, her to attend a Florida beauty academy. She had no contact with either. Her maternal grandparents, who had raised her, were both gone now. As far as he knew, his mother hadn't gone to their funerals or been back to Lubec for any reason since moving to Eastport shortly before he was born. That was all the family history he had been able to extract from her.

So, with a little luck, no one would ever find out, he'd told himself. He'd finish high school, and he'd move, and the secret was something he'd leave behind forever.

Which was the reason he'd decided to break up with Susan.

Too many times he'd seen guys who had planned to leave pulled back by a girl. Sometimes it was the honest demands of the heart. More often, though, she was pregnant, and long-held plans to join the Air Force or find a job at Bath Iron Works or even to go to college were suddenly canceled. The young couple would wed in a quick ceremony, move into a cheap rental, and begin their married lives struggling for a place in the bleak Downeast economy.

Sometimes the boys had been high-school athletes, and in the winter, they'd show up religiously for the alumni basketball game. For the first few years, they'd strive mightily to win, to show everyone that this year's crop of athletes hadn't quite displaced last year's stars in the game that held the town's heart.

But once a few years had passed, cigarettes and beer guts started to take their toll, and then the competition no longer seemed as important as reminiscing about ever-more-distant glories, about game-winning baskets scored, about legendary powerhouses nearly upset, about tournaments played in frantic finishing runs that were forever frozen in their memories.

Not him. He wouldn't let that happen. Once graduation came, he'd be gone.

And that meant ending things with Susan while it was still easy. They hadn't had sex yet, but they had been moving steadily toward it. Teenagers their age did, plenty of them. Eastport was a small, poor town, with too much drinking and too little diversion and with horizons that pressed in so close that adult life seemed to begin the day high school ended, and in that world, it made little sense to wait. It was the rare senior girl who wasn't sleeping with her boyfriend, and it wasn't so very unusual for juniors or sophomores, either.

Susan was his first girlfriend, someone he'd never have dreamed of being with if it hadn't just happened. He knew her a little because she sat across from him in algebra, but only enough to exchange a "hi" or borrow a pen or pencil from.

But she was in the passenger seat of Tari Clark's car, which had a pickup idling next to it, when he'd walked by on the breakwater one fog-chilled June night. He'd seen the two girls there before, chatting with various high-school friends who pulled alongside to check in with Tari, who was a class ahead and popular with everyone.

Susan waved, and he'd arched his eyebrows and mouthed a "hi."

She was out of car, walking toward the end of the pier, when he turned and started back.

"Hi, Dan."

"Hey, Susan."

"What's doing?"

"Not much. You look cold."

"Yeah."

"So why are you outside?"

"Tari is having a flirt-a-thon with Jimmy Tuttle. I felt like an old nun sitting there chaperoning." She pushed her head toward him and let her expression grow stern and disapproving, then giggled.

Tuttle was a junior with an indolent grin and a double-entendre-laden sense of humor that was suggestive without quite being lewd.

"You want my coat?"

She shook her head no, though he could tell she did.

"I just need to move. Can I come with you?"

They walked down the breakwater, turned left, and went along Water Street to Bank Square. She was shivering by then.

"Take my coat. Really."

"Then you'll be cold."

"Not in this." He tugged at the collar of his L.L.Bean flannel.

"Okay," she said and then, when she had zipped it, added, "Thanks."

When they got back to the car, Jimmy had parked his truck and was in the car with Tari.

He lowered the window as they approached.

"What did she give you for your coat, Dan?"

"Nothing," he said, before realizing Tuttle was joking.

"It's worth a squeeze, I'd say. Maybe even some cleavage squeezage."

Susan wrinkled her nose.

"Which explains why nobody ever wears *your* coat, Jimmy."

"Get in and we'll go for a ride," Tari said.

Jimmy had kept at it while they made a long circuit around town.

"You should get a kiss at least. He deserves one, doesn't he, Susan?"

"If he wants one."

"Woot-woot. Ball's in your court, Dan. Whaddya say?"

He shrugged.

"Maybe you don't think she's pretty."

He said what he thought, what he'd always thought, looking at her dimpled cheeks, her brown eyes, her cascade of chestnut hair.

"She's beautiful."

And suddenly their faces were together, and something he'd never done before was happening, just like that.

"You smell really good," he said when they broke apart. It came out loud in the confines of the car, and he felt like an idiot for saying it. But she just giggled.

"It's the new perfume I got in St. Stephen's."

"Susan puts it everywhere she wants to be kissed."

"You wish, Tari." And then, after a second, "Oh my God, that so didn't come out right."

Suddenly everyone in the car was laughing, and then they were kissing again. No, making out.

When he had finally gotten out of Tari's car a couple of blocks from his house and she and Susan had driven off, he'd balled the barracuda jacket to his nose and inhaled deeply. A year ago, he couldn't have dreamed of affording it, and now it was something a pretty high-school girl had worn as they sat crushed together, her mouth fused to his.

In the first heady weeks of their relationship, it had seemed incredible to him just to have her lips on his, her tongue twisting against his, to feel her breasts pushed against his chest when he pulled her tightly to him.

Then one day, when they were making out in the backseat of Tari's car while she had gone off on a ride with Jimmy, he ran his hands down her shoulder and cupped her breasts. They were still there when Tari and Jimmy returned ten minutes later.

The day he had given her his class ring, she had let him slip a hand beneath her sweater and slide her bra up. Only when her mother had called "Sue, it's getting late" from upstairs did she rearrange herself, giggling conspiratorially as she straightened her clothing and smoothed her hair.

Like any teenage couple, they wanted a place to be alone together, but in Eastport, that was a struggle. Her family had two cars, which meant Susan had regular weekend access to a Subaru Outback, a model so versatile at meeting the demands of Maine's dramatically different seasons that it might as well have been the state's official vehicle. But with the use of the car came the stipulation that she wasn't to take it any further than Quoddy Village, the last Eastport neighborhood. And that made finding privacy for a parking session a problem. The breakwater was too public, the school campuses too regularly checked by the police, the Old Toll Bridge Road, so-called because it had once led to a bridge that connected Eastport to Perry across the narrows of Half Moon Cove, too often the site of high-school drinking parties.

"I know a place," he said one night when other teen-driven cars were occupying all the spots they'd hoped to find vacant.

"In here? With all the dead people. Ick. That's creepy," she said when he directed her to turn onto the narrow lane that led into the western side of the cemetery.

"Nope. Keep going."

She drove slowly along until they had passed the last row of headstones.

"Up there, where the boulder is."

They went up the gentle hillock until the Subaru's headlights caught the large granite rock perched at its crest, which had been dedicated as a memorial to Eastport citizens who had served in World War II and Korea. He directed her up around the boulder and a hundred feet further on, where the narrow lane curved behind a slight rise wooded with a screen of birch and fir.

"No one ever comes up here at night, and if they did, we'd see them long before they saw us. If they come in the way we did, we just keep on this road and go out the far end. If someone drives toward us from that direction, all you gotta do is go back to the boulder and keep going straight, and you eventually end up behind the elementary school and go out that way."

She turned the car off and turned toward him.

"I didn't even know this was here," she said, and then added in a suggestive tone, "but I guess you've spent a *lot* of time up here."

No, he said, truthfully. After baseball practice, he sometimes climbed the rock outcropping on the first-base side of the diamond and angled his way home through the cemetery. When you went that way, the memorial was almost the first thing you encountered.

In the make-out sessions there that finished a Friday or Saturday evening, he was soon unbuttoning her blouse and undoing her bra almost as a matter of course. One night, as they lay side by side on the car's reclining passenger seat, he moved his hand down over the gentle curve of her stomach, sliding his fingers slowly inside the slack waist of her beltless jeans until they were under the edge of her underwear. At that point, she had stopped him, but given how far he had gotten, the message was not no, but not yet.

Then came the mid-December day when her parents went to

Bangor Christmas shopping and left her home. He had asked several times for a picture of her in a bikini. It was a fad on the team: Most of the seniors had photos of their girlfriends in skimpy suits, tanned and shiny with body oil, taped inside their lockers.

"I don't have any pictures like that," she had said, then, seeing his look, "Oh, poor Dan. Maybe when the summer comes."

That Saturday afternoon, as they sat in her family's rec room, there next to her own basement bedroom, he had a happy inspiration.

"We could take the bikini picture."

"If I had a bikini."

"You have bikini underwear."

"No way. What if someone stole your phone?"

He'd summoned up all his teenage longing for his next gambit.

"I'd settle for a look."

"Oh you would?"

"I would."

"And stop all the talk about the picture?"

"At least till summer."

"More like, till next week."

But he could tell the idea intrigued her.

"Would you be good?"

"What's good?"

"Sitting right there on the couch and not getting up while I'm . . . modeling."

"Okay."

"Promise?"

"Promise."

With that, she rose and shut off the overhead light so the room was lit only by the floor lamp beside the couch, then reached behind him and, with a little laugh, turned up the thermostat.

"I don't want to be all goose-bumpy," she said, disappearing into her room.

He sat there marveling at what was about to happen, sat so long he half thought she had changed her mind. Then some music, a dance beat, started. It grew abruptly louder as her door opened.

"Okay, Dan, take your mental picture."

With that, she danced slowly toward him. Her dark brown hair was combed forward, and swayed on the top of her breasts, which bounced gently in a satiny blue bra. He looked quickly to her bare feet, then brought his glance greedily up her slim legs to her knees, her thighs, the tantalizing blue of her bikini underwear.

She was in front of him now, and she twirled slowly around, making it hard to study her as closely as he wanted.

"Put your hands in your pockets, and you can have a kiss."

He did, and she lowered herself onto his lap. She raised her arms, draped them slowly around his neck so her breasts pressed flat against him, then brought her mouth to his.

"How about taking your top off?"

"Uh-uh. Not part of the deal."

"C'mon. It's not like I haven't seen them."

"Then why do you need to see them again?" she teased.

"It'd be special this way. Something to dream about."

"You are so bad," she said, frowning in mock reproach. She stood and walked back into her room. After a few seconds, the door opened again.

"Are you still on the couch?"

"Yup."

At that, she came back into the room, her arms tightly crossed in front of her. She sashayed up and down the room, like a model on a catwalk, then stopped in front of him and dropped her hands to her sides. He watched, mesmerized, as she twirled slowly in front of him, naked but for a thin band of cotton, a vision of loveliness written in tight teenage lines.

"Give me another kiss."

She pranced his way, raising one arm teasingly across her breasts, then put her hands on the top of the couch and leaned forward to meet his lips. Their mouths fused together, and he put his arm around her waist, pulled her down to him.

"Dan, no."

"C'mon. Just for a minute." His voice was ragged. "Please."

"Stop it."

Pushing hard against him, she twisted free, scrambled to her feet, and ran to her room.

He had sat for a second, feeling her absence like physical pain, and then followed her there. She was near her bed, pulling on her jeans. When she saw him, she brought her arms up across her naked breasts. His left arm was around her waist now, and he pulled her body tight to his.

"Dan, stop it."

She tried to twist away, but he had his other arm up high, his hand on her cheek, and he turned her face toward his. Now his mouth was on hers.

She sunk her teeth into his lip, and he jerked back.

"Let go or I'll scream."

He tried again to kiss her.

"Nooooo. Stop. *Stop!*"

Her shriek rang in his ears, jolted him, and he felt his grip go slack.

He stood there looking at her, hands at his sides, his self-control only then coming back.

"Get out of my room. Go, Dan. Right now."

She had her phone in her hand.

"If you don't go, I'm calling the police."

He backed through the door. She pushed it closed behind him.

He stood there for a minute, unsure of what to do.

"Susan."

She didn't reply.

"Susan, I'm sorry. Please come out."

"No. I want you to go."

He tried to turn the knob, but the door was locked.

"I said I'm sorry. Can we talk?"

"Not now. Maybe in a couple days. But right now, you need to go."

CHAPTER 14

AND SO HE'D left. And he hadn't called.

She had, a week or so later, sounding both hurt and uncertain. He was downstairs doing homework when his phone rang. Seeing her number, he climbed the stairs to his room as he answered.

"Dan, are we ever going to talk?"

"About what?"

"About us."

"Let's just leave it where it is."

"You mean, like, over?"

"I guess."

"Just because . . . because of what happened?"

"Yeah."

"I'm not mad at you. It just scared me. Come over, and we'll go for a walk."

"I'd better not."

"Why not?"

He launched into the spiel he had run through so many times in his head.

"You should be with somebody better, Susan. I'm not good enough for you. We both know that."

"I don't think that," she said, her voice starting to break. "Really, I don't. And I don't want you to."

But he wouldn't budge.

"Trust me, Susan, someday you'll thank me."

CHAPTER 15

HE SAT DOWN on the twin bed that had been his for as long as he could remember. How many other nights had he lain here in this room, falling asleep to the Red Sox on the radio, Fenway Park seeming as distant and magical as the Taj Mahal? And now he had been there, not once, but half a dozen times, sitting with his teammates in the bleachers, shivering in the spring chill or soaking up the September sun, laughing and joking nonchalantly, as though there was nothing unusual about it.

His eyes fell on the Shead Tigers baseball schedule taped to the wall beside the bed. He had penciled in the score for all the games up to the one in Lubec.

Lubec no longer operated its own high school, so much had its population shrunk. Instead, its several dozen teenagers were enrolled at Washington Academy, half an hour away in East Machias. But as a goodwill gesture and to build fans and loyalty, Washington Academy had agreed to play some of their games in Lubec, and the contest with Eastport was one such match.

The one where it all started.

He had been pitching in the bottom of the seventh. There were no outs, but he was working a batter who was hanging on to a full count only by fouling off his curve.

He'd been throwing well, but now a breeze was kicking up off the water, bringing with it the rotten-egg smell of low tide. He wound up and sent his fastball hurling at the inside corner. As soon as the ball had left his hand, he felt the subtle sense that resides in a pitcher's fingertips, telling him he'd missed. Close, but too far inside. So now there'd be a man on.

But the umpire stepped from behind the plate and cocked his right hand.

"You're out."

A gift.

From the stands there had been a chorus of boos. And then the cry, from the area over behind third base. At first, he thought it was "ape"—that they were mocking his appearance.

Then it came again, and this time, he heard the low, sustained *Raaayyy* that started the chant.

Raaape. Raaaaaape. Raaaaaaaaape.

The next batter came to the plate. He got a quick strike, missed with a changeup, then wound up and threw a big overhand curve that broke hard, zigging inside for a called strike he wasn't totally sure he'd earned.

This time, he felt the cry like a slap the second it started.

Raaaaaaaaaape.

Mr. Healey always said to never let hecklers know they've gotten inside your head, but as he shook off a sign from Frank Cummings, the catcher, he couldn't help looking in the direction of the chant.

Three men who appeared to be in their late thirties or early forties, two with cans of beer in their hands, were sitting on lawn chairs in the back of a pickup parked behind a squat metal industrial building just beyond the field. One, seeing him glance their way, mouthed something to the others. As soon as he turned his attention back to the batter, the cry came again.

Now he found himself waiting for the chant. His next throw was to be an inside fastball, usually one of his best pitches, but it left his hand wrong, and a second later, he heard the sharp crack of a bat making solid contact. The ball caromed deep into center field for a double.

Cummings called for a curve to start the next batter. He wound up, but his grip felt wrong. The ball came in high and wide. The catcher lunged, but it eluded his glove and sent him running toward the backstop. The runner advanced.

Mr. Healey came out to the mound.

"You okay, Danny?"

"I dunno."

"We need this one. Can you find the groove again?"

He looked down at his feet.

"You want out?"

He'd never willingly left a game before, even when his arm was so thrown out it felt like lead, but now he wanted nothing so much as the anonymity of the bench.

"Maybe I'd better."

Healey nodded, a perplexed look on his face.

"Okay."

Amos Pottle, a lanky lefthander from upcountry, came to the mound. The next few batters weren't strong hitters, and Pottle was throwing well.

From the dugout, he watched every pitch, anticipating the called strikes, waiting, hoping, for the ragging to start. For the chant to come again. Loud cheers and boos did, from the same spot, each time something went right, or wrong, for the Washington Academy squad.

But not that mocking jeer.

He surveyed the area from the shelter of the dugout, squinting into the distance of the bright day, but all he could see were head and shoulders in profile against the afternoon sun.

He made his way to the far side of the dugout and then out to the edge of the diamond. The angle was better from there. It was a red short-bed pickup with black exhaust pipes that rose along the back edge of the cab, then leveled into foot-long flanges, whose purpose was to direct the unmuffled noise of the engine back and to the sides.

When a Washington Academy batter was thrown out at first, he was surprised to find the game was over. But for his teammate's congratulatory high fives, he wouldn't have known who had won, for his thoughts were locked on the box in the attic.

CHAPTER 16

HE HAD THOUGHT about going to Lubec to ask about the red pickup with the cutaway pipes; if the owner lived locally, people would know him.

But what would he do then?

He knew what he wanted to do: Smash its windows and slash its tires. But if that was his mission, it precluded asking around town about the owner.

The very act of inquiring would pique interest in him, and that meant people would take careful note of his appearance and watch him as he walked away to see whether he'd arrived by car or ferry or bike. Even if he could coax his mother into letting him use the car for a trip he couldn't convincingly explain, he'd have to park it where it wouldn't be noticed and walk into downtown Lubec to make his inquiries.

But what if he went to seek information and not vengeance? If he did find the man, or men, could he really ask why they had yelled what he was sure he had heard?

Perhaps they had been Fortin's Lubec friends who had served on the USS *Saturn*. If so, would he want to identify himself? Or answer their possible questions about his mother?

Besides, would anyone who would yell such a thing tell him anything helpful?

And so, the weekend had passed without him doing anything.

And then, everything changed.

He had known all along that rendering it all real again would mean revisiting the spot where it had happened.

He walked down the stairs and stopped at the kitchen table to retrieve the keys. The keys—why did he care? What was the sense of locking the place? There was absolutely nothing there worth anything.

The air carried the sharp briskness of an early-spring coastal evening, and he zipped his jacket against it and jammed his hands in the pockets. He walked back up through narrow North End roads and then along High Street into the cemetery. When he came to the last of the small macadam cemetery lanes, he walked to the plaque-marked granite boulder that served as the town's war memorial.

It made him think of Susan—her shirt unbuttoned, her bra off, the sweet gardenia smell of her Hawaiian shampoo, their ragged breathing as they made out. She'd been his first girlfriend, his only real girlfriend before Hannah. He wondered if she knew he was out now, that he was at Bates. What would he say if he ran into her while he was home? Probably best to say nothing, he decided, nothing beyond a nodded hello.

Leaving the memorial behind, he walked the lane, really no more than two pebbled tire paths separated by a sod center, that led up the rise toward the granite outcropping that, from a height of fifty feet or so, overlooked the high-school baseball diamond. He stood there for a few minutes gazing out over the early evening lights of the town and beyond them to the encircling bays that had, before the construction of a causeway, left Eastport an island.

Making his way down the rocks, he went to the pitcher's mound and surveyed home plate for a moment, then walked the hard-packed dirt surface until he came to the broad school-bus lane that circled in front of the elementary school.

The three of them had been sitting there at a picnic table at the far end of the school's small blue-and-green jungle-gym playground—probably because there were no clear sightlines from either the elementary school or, across High Street, the high school, making it a good place to smoke unobserved.

He'd given them a quick glance as he'd walked from baseball practice back toward the high school but without any sort of acknowledgment. He didn't count any of the three as a friend nor they him.

Kimball was the only one he really knew. The older boy had been a good starting pitcher the previous year, the season his own speed and spin had come together with an alchemy that seemed almost magical. A lanky kid with a solid fastball and a deceptive changeup, he wasn't a dazzler the way his brother Bobby had been on the basketball court, but he was a smart, dependable player, one who had the tools to win when the team's bats were connecting.

Yet when his own pitches were working, when he was in the zone, Dan was better, able to mow down another squad's sluggers with a curve that left them lunging or a fastball that found that flummoxing groove at the low inside edge of the strike zone. By late season, he and not Kimball was regularly being chosen for must-win games.

Reserved to start with, Kimball had grown even more distant toward him, his previous "How ya doin'?" fading to the briefest of nods when they passed each other and then to the pretense that he hadn't noticed Dan at all. He had finished out the season, then decided not to play his final year. Too much fun stuff to do as a senior, he'd told other teammates. Not that those supposed diversions had kept him from being a spectator at some of the team's games.

He could hear the three laughing snidely.

"Hey, Winters."

He'd looked over again.

"Yeah?"

"From what I heard over in Lubec, it sounds like Susan Jameison is getting your hardball high and inside—whether she wants it or not."

He charged the instant Kimball had finished delivering his taunt. He wasn't aware of even thinking about it. Three feet out, he launched himself, catching his antagonist square in the gut with his head.

He went down hard, his breath escaping with an *oomph*.

Dan was on his feet by the time Kimball, gasping for breath, had made it to all fours. One hard step forward, and he caught him in the ribs with a kick that sent the taller teen collapsing back to the ground.

"Jesus," Jimmy Emery said.

He turned toward them, but they held their ground.

This time he let Kimball get up, but as soon as he'd regained his feet, gasping and wheezing and signaling by his unguarded stance that the fight was out of him, he sent a fist smashing to his mouth, then another to his nose.

He felt the nose pop, saw the blood come.

When Kimball raised his hands to his face, he caught him in the stomach with an uppercut. The senior fell to his knees, then collapsed on his stomach.

"He's had enough." It was Beal. "You've had enough, right, Griff?"

Kimball mumbled a choked "Yeah."

"You wanna be next, Beal?"

Beal took a step back.

"I got no problem with you. But—"

"Then shut the fuck up."

He grabbed Kimball by his hair, pulled his head up, slammed his face back to the ground, then yanked it up again. His eyes were rolling and unfocused, his mouth a bleeding rictus.

"What'd you hear?"

"Just . . . just some trash talk." Blood gushed from Kimball's nose as he spoke.

"What was it?"

"Nothing, really."

He balled his fist and put it a foot from Kimball's face.

"Tell me what you fucking heard."

"Some older dudes were talking about your old lady and how . . . how she got raped."

"Talking to you about it?"

Kimball tried to shake his head, which was difficult, since Dan had it pulled back tight.

"No. To themselves. They were watching the game and drinking in the back of their truck. I just heard them."

"Who were they?"

"I got no idea. Honest to God."

"Who have you told that to?"

"Nobody. I mean, just uh, uh . . ."

"These two."

"Yeah."

"If you ever say anything like that again, I swear, I'll kill you. I will kill you. And if you ever tell a single fucking person, I will kill you. One single person. You understand?"

"I won't. I won't."

He gave Kimball's head another vicious push into the gravel, then turned to the others.

"You assholes, too. If you ever say a word—a single fucking word—I'll come after you. One single fucking thing. You got me?"

They answered with numb nods.

He turned his back contemptuously and walked away, his legs trembling and his gut churning. He barely made it out of sight behind the high school before he dropped to his knees and succumbed to a searing nausea that left him, too, struggling for air.

He knew he was supposed to regret the explosion of violence, the viciousness of his attack on Kimball—to feel genuinely sorry about the injuries he had inflicted and resolve that he'd never lose his temper like that again, no matter what the provocation was.

But standing there where it had happened, reliving the events in longer moments than they had taken to occur, what he really regretted was that he hadn't slammed a punch into Beal's nose as well. Or knocked that mocking look off his face by smashing his head, too, into the gravel.

CHAPTER 17

HIS MOTHER HAD been in bed when the police cruiser rolled to a stop in the narrow street and the two officers came crunching up the gravel way. Their budget perpetually strained, the Eastport police usually patrolled alone, so having two of them on the stoop immediately signaled that they viewed this situation as different from the other incidents that occasionally brought one of the town's teenagers to their attention.

One was the chief himself, Mel Tolland, whom he knew from the occasional times Tolland, so tall and angular that he seemed to fold himself into the cruiser, had driven the baseball team to away games. His interactions with the town's young people usually carried an air of affectionate amusement, but today he looked down sternly from narrowed eyes.

"Hello, Dan. Is your mother home?"

"She's in bed."

"You'd better wake her up."

But he could already hear her rustling in her bedroom.

"What is it, Danny?"

"It's the police, Mom."

"Oh, dear God. Wait till I put on my housecoat."

A minute later, she appeared, a quilted robe long faded from yellow to dirty beige buttoned all the way to her chin.

"Chief Tolland. What's the matter?"

"Dan hasn't told you?"

He hadn't. He hadn't even seen her. The truth was, he had stayed away until after nine o'clock, when she retired to her room on nights free of church functions.

"Danny, what's wrong?"

"I got into a little fight."

Tolland's forehead wrinkled in a frown, lowering his jet-black eyebrows into an almost unified line over his eyes.

"It wasn't a little fight. He gave Griff Kimball one hell of a beating."

"He started it."

"His friends say you charged him."

"Because he was mouthing off."

"Dan, you beat the bloody bejesus out of him. Broke his nose, cracked some ribs, and damn near busted his head open. They had to take him to the Calais hospital."

"Danny, tell me it's not true."

"He's bigger than me. And he was ragging me."

"None of that matters a hill of beans. You can't pound someone half to death just because he annoys you."

The chief turned to his mother.

"The Kimballs are pressing charges. We're going to have to take him in. Do you want to come to the station with him, ma'am?"

His mother's hands were folded in front of her, her head bowed. Her lips were moving, and he caught the murmur of the words he had heard so many times before.

". . . Thy will be done, on Earth as it is in Heaven. And give us this day our daily bread, and forgive us . . ."

There had been no thought of a lawyer. They had no money, and when the chief had suggested Pine Tree Legal, the State's legal services association, his mother had been resistant.

"If we just trust in God, it will be okay."

So there had been no negotiation, no deal, none of that.

When the judge in Calais District Court asked him how he pled to the count of aggravated assault and battery, he had answered what he believed to be true.

"Not guilty, Your Honor."

And so there had been a trial of sorts. The assistant district attorney had called the emergency room doctor to the stand and had him describe, in grave medical terms, the injuries Griff Kimball had sustained.

"Would you say these are the sort of things that come from a normal schoolboy scrape?"

"No," the young doctor replied. "This is the kind of beating you see when the assailant is bent on causing real injury."

Next came Kimball, Sonny Beal, and Jimmy Emery, all of whom, under questioning, gave short accounts of the incident, careful to avoid his eyes as they did.

Then the judge had called him to the stand.

"Now, Mr. Winters, you don't have to answer me if you don't want to, as you have a Fifth Amendment right not to incriminate yourself, but this is juvenile court, and I'm only trying to understand this case as best I can, so I can do what I think is right. Rest assured, I know something about teenage scrapes. I had a few myself back in the day. But this seems to go beyond that, and the State is treating it as a very serious matter. So I'd like to hear your side of the story but only if you want to tell it. Would you like to say something in your defense?"

"I was minding my own business, and he started mocking me."

"But you initiated the physical altercation, did you not?"

"I had to teach him a lesson."

"You beat him pretty badly. The witnesses say you kicked him when he was on the ground and that you drove his head into the ground when he was no longer fighting back. After he said he'd had enough, in fact. Why didn't you stop when he gave up?"

He sat mute.

"Well, then, can you tell me what he said that made you so enraged that you administered a beating that put Mr. Kimball in the hospital for five . . . am I right here?"—a nod from the prosecution bench, and he continued—"for five days?"

"He said something about my old girlfriend."

"What?"

"I don't remember, exactly, Your Honor."

"You don't remember?"

"No, sir."

"And this was an old girlfriend?"

"Yes, sir."

"How old?"

"She's seventeen, Your Honor."

The judge shook his head impatiently. "I mean, how long since she's been your girlfriend?"

"We broke up in January, Your Honor."

"So let me see if I have this straight. You beat this young man badly enough to hospitalize him because he said something too inconsequential to remember about a girl you no longer go out with?"

He said nothing.

"Is that a correct summation?"

"I . . . I guess."

"Now I'd like to hear from Mr. Kimball again," the judge said.

The senior shuffled back to the stand, where he sat staring at his hands.

"Am I correct in saying Mr. Winters continued to assault you after you made it clear you'd had enough, Mr. Kimball?"

"Well, sort of. But fights happen. If it was up to me, I wouldn'ta said anything. But my folks—"

"I understand the high-school code of honor. Everyone would rather die than be a snitch. But a serious assault took place here, and that's a crime."

"He's right, though. I started it."

"Did you hit him first?"

"No, but I was talking trash to him."

"Then maybe you can tell us what you said that precipitated this whole incident. Since Mr. Winters seems to have forgotten."

"I don't remember, exactly."

"Take a minute and try to recall for us, Mr. Kimball."

Griff shifted in the witness chair, looked at the ceiling, frowned.

"I think I said his ex-girlfriend was a slut, Your Honor."

CHAPTER 18

SUSAN HAD COME to see him the weekend before he had to leave for the Long Creek Youth Development Center, as Maine's juvenile prison was called. It was the first time they had spoken face-to-face since that afternoon in her basement. Although he had continued to mouth an uncertain "hi" when he saw her in the hall, she had passed in tight-lipped silence, sometimes pretending not to notice him at all.

But everyone now knew what had happened in court, what Griff had told the judge had started the fight, and that had made her magnanimous. Maybe she was touched by the thought of him defending her even though they were no longer together.

Or perhaps now that he was being sent away, she'd decided he really had been self-denying and sincere in saying she was too good for him. Maybe now that time had eased the hurt, his renunciation made him seem both damned and noble.

"I feel so terrible about you being in all this trouble because you stood up for me," she said. "I mean, I'm flattered and all, but I don't care if Griff Kimball called me a slut. Anybody who hangs out with Sonny Beal has something seriously wrong with him. I wish you'd just ignored him."

He nodded.

"I should have. But I just couldn't."

"It's so awful that you're being sent away. Will you write me from . . . from school?"

Again, he nodded. It was easier than saying no.

She leaned forward and kissed his cheek. As she pulled away, he saw the tears in her eyes.

"I feel so bad," she said. "All because of me."

It wasn't. Griff had told the judge that he had called her a slut, and Dan hadn't contradicted him. But that wasn't what he'd really said. Not even close. Remembering it now, he could feel rage start to rise within him.

CHAPTER 19

THE QUESTIONS THE judge had asked were the same things Dr. Pratt homed in on during his twice-a-month counseling sessions at Long Creek.

"The fight isn't the reason you're here," the psychiatrist said. "It's the kind of beating you gave him. We need to figure out why you did that."

"Because I lost it."

"That's what I mean. We need to figure out *why* you lost it."

He liked Dr. Pratt. A large bald man with sympathetic eyes and a quick laugh, he was a good listener, nodding as his patient described growing up poor, wincing as he relayed the barbs he'd endured from other kids. It was the therapist who had suggested, after six months of sessions, that he apply to Bates.

"Why would they take somebody like me?"

"You're right. They wouldn't. Forget it. You're a loser. Let's try to get you into a tough prison instead."

He looked over, puzzled, from the couch.

"Huh?"

"What I mean, Dan, is quit feeling sorry for yourself and listen to somebody who knows more than you do. And who happens to be a trustee there."

"But I'm serious. Why would they want me?"

"Because liberals believe in redemption, and liberals run the colleges. And because it's the kind of thing that lets college administrators feel good about themselves. And because your grades are pretty respectable. And last but not least, because I hear you can do things with a baseball that make coaches salivate. But all I can do is open the door for you. You'll have to persuade them."

"How?"

"Start by acknowledging that you messed up, then talk about the progress you've made here. They've got to feel confident that you won't go knocking the stuffing out of some rich twit from Connecticut, because those kids are their bread and butter. Then I'd talk about how Bates can help you realize your dreams."

"Like what?"

"They're your dreams, Dan. What do you want to do with your life?"

"I don't know."

"Well, what do you think about when you contemplate the future?"

"Getting out of here."

"Beyond that."

"Maybe joining the service."

"Why?"

"Because they'd probably take me, despite everything. And I don't want to go back to Eastport."

Dr. Pratt slapped the arm of his chair in frustration.

"You've got to get up off the mat, Dan. You screwed up, but this isn't the end of your life. What do you want to be? A computer whiz? A lawyer? A teacher? Think about it. If you've given up on yourself, how can you expect anyone else to take a chance on you?"

But as much as he liked Dr. Pratt, he couldn't bring himself to talk truthfully about the fight, because he simply couldn't bring himself to disclose the secret of his own paternity. And so, he had dissembled, saying, as he had to the judge, that he couldn't recall Griff's exact words.

"It was something about her being a slut and me . . . well, putting it to her hard. Sue's a really nice girl, and the way they were all sneering and laughing just got me going."

He did offer up another time, though, an explosion of temper in which there had been no animate victim except himself. That had come after Jennifer Sawyer had confided apologetically that she had had to cut him from her birthday party guest list because her parents said he and his mother belonged to a church of "holy rollers."

"I'm not part of that," he said. "I don't even go."

And he didn't. He had come to view skeptically the church's notion of a father-like God watching closely over the day-to-day activities of its congregants. Did they really have a special relationship with God? How could He actually monitor the activities of each and every one of the more than seven billion people on Earth?

"I can't sit there and pretend someone is watching over the world— not with all the awful stuff that happens," he'd told his mother. "If so, He sure misses an awful lot. The whole concept is dumb."

Where had he gotten that idea, she had wanted to know, as though she worried that a satanic recruiter was somehow whispering corrosive heresies into his ear.

In fact, he had come across it in the school library when researching a paper on George Washington's personal code of conduct, his so-called *Rules of Civility & Decent Behavior*. One article had mentioned that he, like several other prominent founders, was strongly influenced by Deism. This meant that at most, Washington probably believed only in a distant and indifferent God and not one whose messages could be received by extended arms or fluttering fingers or whose sudden spiritual touch would inspire one to speak gibberish or shake or twirl spasmodically or throw one's head back and howl hallelujahs.

That explanation had surprised her—and her reaction, in turn, had surprised him. She hadn't quit speaking to him or demanded that he apologize to the Lord, as she had done when he was younger. Instead, she had pursed her lips and contemplated him for a long moment before speaking.

"Okay, then, Dan," she had finally said. "You can take a break from church, on one condition: You must promise me you won't completely close your mind or your heart to the possibility of the Lord."

And so, he had made that promise and quit attending church.

But once he had told Jennifer that he wasn't part of his mother's church, he was left feeling that he had abased himself in the hope of getting her to try to coax an invitation out of her religiously bigoted parents. The shame he felt for the church and chagrin for that shame collided like wave swash and backwash.

He related to Dr. Pratt how his resentment had built until it was an anger that gripped him and how he had gone that Monday to the Masonic Temple, knowing Jennifer's father was a proud member— how he had intended to key the paint of the new Ford F-150 her father took such pride in but how, instead, he had found himself slamming his fists into the driver's-side window until it had erupted in a series of cracks and how he had kept punching until the glass had given way and pebbled into the cab, leaving his knuckles sore and bleeding.

"I didn't even know what I was doing," he said. "It was like I wasn't in control of my own body. I barely felt like I was me."

That wasn't true. He had known, but he had been determined to break the window, to do something Mr. Sawyer couldn't help noticing, and to that end, he had forced himself to punch through the pain until the window gave way.

But what he told Pratt *did* describe the way he had felt in the fight with Kimball, which meant that he was giving the psychiatrist what he wanted, if only in a roundabout fashion.

The moment, however transposed, was real, and talking about the uncontrolled fury had let him confide to the psychiatrist how he had come to be haunted by dread of that feral self. And that, too, was true.

CHAPTER 20

THE RINGING OF the phone jolted him from his thoughts.

"Dan, this is Reverend Peevers. I hope you're holding up in this moment of great tribulation."

"I'm okay."

"Which is as well as any of us are doing in this sad time when the good Lord has seen fit to call your dear mother to Heaven. I just wanted to check to see that you'd made it home."

"I got here this afternoon."

"Well, visiting hours, as I'm sure you know, are tomorrow afternoon from three to six at Grantley's Funeral Home. And the funeral is Friday morning at eleven, here at the church, of course. Do you want to speak at the service, Dan? Just a few words to tell the congregation what a loving mother our dear Clara was to you?"

"I'm not good at that."

"You mustn't let that be a hurdle. In situations like these, people don't expect polished oratory. They simply want to hear what's in your heart."

"I'm not sure I want to share that."

"Well, why don't you give it some thought? People always like to hear from the family. It makes a funeral service complete. Perhaps you could write out a few pages of recollections. It would be my honor to give voice to the sentiments of a son silenced by grief. After all, the Lord himself has many messengers."

Too many, Dan thought to himself.

"I will."

He put the phone back in its cradle on the wall and opened the refrigerator. There was peanut butter there—why had his mother always insisted on refrigerating it?—as well as a jar of blackberry jam. He made a sandwich, devoured it, and went back for another.

He wandered back up the stairs, but this time, he turned the opposite way, into her bedroom. A faded blue comforter was pulled over the bed, the pillow angling out from its far edge. A beige blouse lay across the blanket, as though she had just ironed it and planned to put it on. The two Bibles were in their accustomed places.

Sitting on her dresser in a plastic frame was a photo he hadn't seen before. The two of them, standing side by side in front of the house. One of her arms was around his waist, the other rested on his left shoulder. He held his own body rigidly and was leaning away, his lips giving a faint hint of a forced smile.

When had they . . . oh yes, just after he had arrived home from his furlough the Thanksgiving before last. After walking half the night on the way back from Holden Mills. On the way back from seeing his father.

"Look at you, Danny, just look at you. You're such a handsome young man. I'm going to get Mrs. Goodell to take our picture."

The need to confront his inner fears, the fears he couldn't confide even to Dr. Pratt, had led him to the block of small, weather-beaten houses in Holden Mills. He had risked a lot by going. Released on a four-day-holiday furlough from the Center, he was supposed to take the Downeast bus straight home for the Thanksgiving weekend and to notify the Eastport police when he arrived.

Instead, he had boarded a bus that went even further north, into the Maine hinterland. If they found out, he'd say he had raced to get something to eat when the bus stopped in Bangor, that it had left without him, and that he'd had to hitchhike home. But even if it cost him the privileges he had won through good behavior and diligent schoolwork, even if it ruined his chances for early release, he had to know.

The wind came cold and raw under a zinc-gray sky, a wind made worse by the heavy sulfur stench of paper company it carried. He had already walked by four times, inspections separated by circuitous courses through the blighted neighborhood. And yet, he couldn't make himself go up the worn path to the front door. Just two first-floor windows punctuated the house's green asphalt exterior, and no light was visible either there or from the second-floor window set between the sharp rake of the roof.

Just do it. Go to the door and knock. There's probably no one there anyway.

And what if there is? What do I say? I'm your son. You raped my mother. I had to see what you're like, so I can know who I am?

That was the truth of it—the reason he'd been determined to make the trip from the moment a friend whose good behavior had earned him unsupervised Internet access had found the address for him. Didn't Fortin owe him that?

He started up the path. As he did, a short-haired black mongrel appeared from around the corner of the house, dragging a long, frayed rope.

The dog climbed the stoop and stood there watching him.

He took a step forward. The dog growled halfheartedly.

Slinging his backpack off his right shoulder, he retrieved the roast beef sub he had gotten from the Center's cafeteria and peeled back the cellophane. He pulled out a large piece of the meat.

"Here, boy."

At first, the dog seemed curious. But when he raised his arm to dangle the roast beef in front of him, it kiyied in panic and scurried behind the house, so he stuffed the slice of meat into his own mouth. Like all the Center's food, it was overcooked, but even so, the taste of roast beef and horseradish mustard was surprisingly good.

He put the sub back in his pack, then mounted the two wooden steps and knocked before he could talk himself out of it. After a minute or so, he knocked again, louder. But there was nothing, and with a sense of disappointment commingled with relief, he started back off the stoop.

The dog had crept back to the corner of the house and stood there, eyeing him.

He got the sub out again, peeled off the cellophane, ripped off perhaps a quarter of the long roll, and held it forward, low and slow.

"Here you go, killer."

The dog appraised him, desire battling fear.

He tossed it underhand toward the animal. Gaze shifting between him and the food, the dog crept forward, then snatched the roll in its mouth and retreated a safe distance to gulp it down.

"Come have some more."

The creature took a few steps, then stopped and stood waiting.

He tossed the next piece in a high arc, and the dog caught it in midair.

Now he crouched and held out the fat remaining piece, full of cold cuts and cheese. Tail wagging slowly, the dog crept forward until it was just a few feet away.

"That's it, boy." Another step, then it halted and met his eyes imploringly. "Come get it."

Despite all his urgings, however, the dog would advance no farther. Opening his mouth wide, he brought the sandwich slowly toward his face, as though to eat it himself. But the second his arm reached shoulder level, the dog yelped and fled again, once more disappearing around the corner of the small house.

"Some watchdog you are."

The dog reappeared, head poking around the edge of the dwelling to peer at him. After a moment, he laid the sub down in the dead grass and backed slowly away. He hadn't gone more than five paces when the animal seized the stuffed roll and loped back behind the house.

"You looking for somebody?"

Startled, he turned to see a white-haired woman with a shawl over her shoulders leaning out from the half-opened door of the neighboring house.

"For Mr. Fortin."

"Who are you?"

"My name's Dan. I think he knows my father. From the Navy."

"He's never home till late."

"How late?"

"Whenever the American Legion closes."

Again, the hesitation, this time before the door of the American Legion Hall, a two-story brick building a few blocks from downtown.

Come on, do it. The old lady knows; she'll say something, so there's no turning back.

He opened the wooden door with the frosted-glass panels and stepped inside.

There were only eight people in the room, four at the bar, large-bellied men with blue Teamsters jackets or trucking caps, none yet over fifty by his reckoning. Along one wall, three more were clustered at a table, playing cribbage.

And in a far corner, back to them, one figure sat alone in black jeans and a leather Harley-Davidson vest, smoking a cigarette and absently swirling ice in a whiskey tumbler as he stared out the window into the darkening gray.

Looking at the remote figure, an overwhelming desire to leave came over him. He stood a few seconds longer, then swallowed hard and walked to the bar.

The bartender glanced up from the dishwasher he was unloading.

"Don't even try it, kid,"

"I'm looking for somebody."

"Who?"

"Lester Fortin."

"See those men playing cribbage? The one with the glasses."

He moved his gaze back from the solitary smoker. The relief he felt made it easy to walk to the table where the cribbage players sat.

"Excuse me, are you Mr. Fortin?"

The man who looked up at him seemed to be about forty-five, with close-cropped black hair and a paunch starting to settle over his belt.

"Long time since anybody's called me that. I guess you got a car that needs working on?"

"Nope."

"Huh. That's what most young guys come see me for. So what's it with you?"

"Can we talk alone?"

He winked at the other two and rose.

"Excuse me, guys, but I gotta parley with this mysterious stranger." He turned toward Dan. "You probably want to buy me a beer for my time."

"You should buy him one, Bud. He's saving you money by taking you away from the cribbage board." The man guffawed loudly at his own gibe.

"Fuck you, Jim."

Dan dug in his pocket and pulled out one of his three fives.

"Best give that to me, as Dale there wouldn't want money coming from somebody looking as young as you. Find a table that suits you. Want a Coke?"

"I'm good."

But he set one down in front of Dan when he returned.

"Might as well have something. Excuse the hands. They're clean, after a fashion, but when you're a mechanic, the grease never really comes out."

Now Fortin settled back in his seat.

"I didn't get your name."

"Dan."

"Well, Dan, what's on your mind?"

"I think you knew my mother."

The man's eyes narrowed. He slid his mug out so it was foot or so away from him on the table, turning it so the curve opposite the handle rested against his palm.

"Clara Winters. From Lubec."

"Careful what you're doing here," Fortin said.

"I'm not doing anything."

"You sure?"

"Yeah."

"It's not one of those things where you're out to get revenge on the SOB that you think wronged your ma? Because the State sent me away for nine years for that."

"I know."

"You're not packing?"

"Packing?"

"A gun."

Dan shook his head.

"How about if you stand up and take off your coat?"

Dan stood, balled his fall jacket, and tossed it lightly into a nearby chair.

"All right," Fortin said. "So what's on your mind?"

And so he arrived at the moment he had thought about for years, the moment that had loomed as a nightmare he knew he'd have to confront almost since the day he had fitted key to lock and opened his mother's dark secret.

"I'm your son."

CHAPTER 21

"MY . . . SON?"

"My mother had me almost exactly nine months after it happened."

The man raised the mug to his lips, gulped his beer, then worked his jaw from side to side.

"That don't mean shit. She could've had a boyfriend. Or just a . . . a one-time thing."

"She would have told me."

"Maybe, maybe not. People keep lots of secrets."

"If it wasn't you, why would she keep it secret? She'd say who it was, so she could get child support."

"Unless she didn't know."

Dan could feel an annoyed frown transforming his face.

"How could she not know?

His mouth was dry as Saharan sand, so much so that it was hard to speak. He tilted the Coke and washed its cool sweetness around his palate.

Fortin looked at him and shrugged.

"Lots of reasons. Maybe she got around. Free love and all that."

A wave of anger struck like a slap. For a second, he felt like up-ending the table on top of Fortin. He took a deep breath, held it for a second, then forced himself to laugh.

"Free love? In Lubec?"

He and Fortin appraised each other for half a minute, neither of them speaking. If he was going to find out what he wanted, he had to get things back on track. But as he tried to figure out how, a half-smile came to the man's face.

"You know, when I first saw you, it struck me there was something familiar about you, and maybe that's it: You do kinda look like me."

"I saw your yearbook photo and thought the same thing."

"You've been doing your research."

He nodded and tried to will a benign look onto his face.

"I just wanted to know about my father, and she wouldn't say anything, so I did some digging and found out. Then I wanted to see if I looked like you."

For a moment, neither spoke, then Fortin's eyes narrowed.

"Just so's you know, I don't got a Canadian buck to my name."

"I don't want money. I just wanted to meet you. I have some questions I wanted to ask."

"Must be like stepping on a rusty nail, coming all that way for this." He spread his hands in front of him and then brought them toward his chest.

"No. It's . . . I'm just . . ."

Dan trailed off, and after an awkward moment, Fortin spoke again.

"No need to bullshit." He glanced over toward the table where his friends were playing cribbage, then toward the bar, and then back again. "You've got questions, you say. Whatta you want to know?"

Dan took a deep breath and held it. It was now or never.

"Sometimes when I get mad, it's like I'm possessed or something. Like it's not even me, and I can't stop it."

"Yeah?"

"Is it ever that way with you?"

"Can't say as it is."

"Was it ever?"

"Not so's I remember. That's not saying I don't blow my stack sometimes. A couple of weeks back, I whacked my head on the hood of the truck I was working on and let go some curses that would make a pirate blush. But that's part of being a man. And at your age, it's worse, what with hormones and all. Like driving a muscle car."

"So . . . it wasn't like that with my mother?"

"Oh, that's what you're getting at." Fortin reached for his glass and drew off a deep swallow. "You mean, did I go at her like a madman?"

"Yeah."

"You really want to hear this? You're not gonna like it."

"That's okay."

"You're sure?"

Dan nodded.

"Okay. No, it wasn't like that. And it wasn't like she said, neither."

He rubbed his left knuckles with his right hand, like a man absently trying to clean away a stain.

"Understand, I'm not saying I don't deserve some blame. God knows I've wrestled with that. I took her outside and gave her a couple of swallows off my pint, trying to get her drunk. But all the stuff that was said at the trial, the stuff about me jumping out at her and the knife and all that—it was a damn lie. The reason they couldn't find the knife in my gear is that there wasn't any fucking knife. I was walking along with her, and we were both looking for a flat patch of grass, if you get me. We found one, and we did what we both knew we would, and that was that. And then she lied about it, the little . . ."

He bit his lip, raised the mug again, then wiped his mouth on his sleeve.

"Don't get me wrong, I own my share of it. In the joint, the shrinks were always going on about how you gotta level with yourself about what you done, and I see these shows about date rape and how you've gotta stop when a girl says no and all that, and maybe I didn't. I was a Navy man, and we all kinda prided ourselves on being on pussy patrol when we got to port. We wanted what we wanted, and we pressed pretty hard for it."

Now he took his right fingers in his left fist and pulled till each popped with a soft hollow sound.

"You really want to hear this, Dan?" He paused. "You don't mind if I call you that?"

"No. And yeah, I'm sure."

"Okay, then. She did say no. But only after her dress was up and her . . . her knickers were down. I was getting on top, and she said, no, no, don't, my grandparents say they'll kick me out if I get pregnant. But I told her I had a rubber, and I put it on and got to making it happen, and I don't remember her saying no again. If she did, it was just a whisper, not like she meant it. And pretty soon we were both going at it pretty good. And then, something feels a little different, and I've got an idea the rubber's let go, but I don't say nothing because I know she'll say to stop.

"And sure enough, when it's over, it has let go. And she notices it and gets all upset. I say she should go right home and wash the way they do and that I'll give her my address and the phone back at our homeport, and if there's a problem, she can get in touch and I'll send some money. So we go out under a streetlight, and I write all that down and give it to her. By now, she's all hysterical, carrying on about how if her grandparents kick her out, there's no one to take her in, and off she goes."

"And that's it?"

"Until a month or so later, when we put into port for a few days down South and the master-at-arms shows up with a couple of Staties, and they haul me off in cuffs. Maybe by then she knew she was knocked up, so she said whatever she figured she had to. But nobody ever mentioned that she had one in the oven at the trial, and I don't remember her looking like she did. That sure as hell would have stuck with me. Who knows, maybe it was too early to tell. But anyway, like I said, they couldn't show a knife or bruises or anything like that, because there wasn't any. Just her word against mine, and they believed her."

"You must be bitter."

"I was for a while. Nine years is a damn long stretch. And if what I did is rape, half the guys I went to high school with should be locked up instead of riding around in their big fucking pickups, joking about all the tail they got when they was young bucks."

He drained his beer and set the glass back on the table.

"But who the hell knows? The shrinks said to make a fresh start, you had to park your anger in a bucket and come clean with yourself. So what I said to myself was, I sure wanted to have a go with her, and maybe I wasn't listening hard enough to what she was saying. And if rape isn't just ripping her clothes off and holding her down and forcing things, which is what I always thought, if it's also just plowing on ahead when she's playing at no but really means yes, then maybe I *was* guilty."

Fortin paused and aimed a wry smile his way.

"Though if that's the case, I sure the hell wish somebody'd told us back then. But regardless, if that's all rape is, maybe it doesn't matter that she made it sound worse than it was."

"Why wouldn't it matter?"

"'Cause if I was guilty of raping her anyway, maybe how hard I raped her don't make any difference."

"It sure sounds different."

Fortin chuckled.

"You of all people, saying just what the voice inside of me used to say."

He looked over at the table where his friends were at their cribbage game, then turned back to Dan.

"You know, before I got in trouble, I used to think the law was pretty clear. I thought you could just find the right book and look up the crime, and if it didn't say pretty much exactly what you'd done, then you were okay. But that's not the way it is. It's really all about arguing for the jury. My lawyer says I'm an angel, and that if I found a hundred-dollar bill on the sidewalk, I'd spend all day looking for the owner, which is a giant wagonload of crap.

"The other lawyer tells the jury I'm so bad the Devil'd run across the road to get outta my way, and I've been like that all my life. And he pretty much guarantees 'em that if they let me off, the next thing I'll do is go after their daughters. No one's telling anything within a mile of the truth, but they don't give a goddamn. It all just depends on who the jury believes, and like I said, they believed her. So I went to the joint."

"Can I ask you something?"

"Don't tell me you got something else stored up."

Dan laughed.

"No, not like that. This is where you're from, right?"

"Yup."

"Why'd you come back here? Doesn't everybody know?"

"A lot of 'em. But sometimes coming back is all you got. They give you fifty dollars or so and let you out, and you stand there and say, what happens now? After all those years inside, the whole world's changed, and you're kind of lost, and you want to be somewhere familiar, somewhere you know. And by then my old lady had passed away—the old man'd run off years ago—and left me a little house. It's not much, but not much is a lot compared to nothing, which is what I had at the time."

Dan tried to imagine returning to Eastport after having done time for rape, knowing that every person he passed on the street was silently rehashing his crime, that each time he left the WaCo Diner, the fishermen and stevedores and truck drivers would make wisecracks under their breath. It was bad enough as it was, and all he'd done was get into a fight.

"How'd they treat you?"

"Some pretty bad, some halfway decent."

Fortin held up his grease-stained hands.

"Like them, it's pretty much impossible to get rid of once it's there. It made finding a job a tough go. The first couple of years, nobody would give me anything steady. I almost lost my house for taxes, but that spring, the town had a lot of roads redone. The paving company was from out of Bangor and didn't know my past, and they picked me up."

"What do you do now?"

"Some years back, I got on with the Irving out on the interstate. It's a big truck stop, and that's what I was in the Navy, a diesel mechanic. I kind of do it all. Fix trucks, pump gas for them that needs it done for 'em, plow some in the winter."

"Do you have . . . a girlfriend?"

"Nope. Though I'll tell you, it wouldn't be so hard. Women let you know sometimes they're interested, even them that know about it. There's even some that seem to find me more interesting because of it." He shook his head. "Crazy bitches."

"So why don't you?"

"Guess I'm kinda gun-shy."

Dan took another sip of his Coke and tried to think of what more to ask. Fortin spoke before anything else came to mind.

"So how about you? You still in high school?"

"Yeah."

"Senior?"

He nodded.

"Play any sports?"

"Baseball."

"What position?"

"Pitcher."

"Damn. Me too. What's your best pitch?"

"I've got a pretty good curve."

"Really move?"

"When I'm on."

"Good for you. It's goddamn hard to throw a good one."

"I practiced something wicked."

"You gotta, to be good at anything. You know that feeling, when it's all working, and you hitch back and throw, just knowing exactly where the ball's gonna go?"

"Yeah."

"God, that's a great thing. Like magic. So, you get good grades?"

"Pretty good."

"On the honor roll?"

"Sometimes."

Fortin laughed.

"That must be your . . . your mom. I never even came close."

Fortin raised the mug and took another swallow of beer.

"And you're having problems with your temper?"

"Sometimes."

"Like what?"

And slowly, Dan found himself divulging his troubles.

He didn't tell about Kimball, because he didn't want to reveal he was in Long Creek. But he related the fight he had gotten into with Darren Morrison when Morrison had taunted him about the Army Surplus jacket he had thought made him look cool, how his words—"Is that what's hot in poor people's fashion this fall?"—had stung like a whip, how the blood had pounded in his head until the pulse seemed to consume him. How, once the fight started, he hadn't even felt it when the other boy had hit him, had only heard the dull *pock* of the punch landing. How he had drilled his tormenter twice in the jaw. How it had taken two other kids to pull him off.

How he had felt a similar rage when Jennifer Sawyer had told him she was sorry, but she couldn't invite him to her party because her parents said he and his mother were holy rollers and how he had gone that Monday to the Masonic Temple, found her father's new Ford pickup, and slammed his fists into the driver's window until it broke and his knuckles were bleeding.

Fortin sat and listened to his halting recitation.

"Just those times? Nothing since?"

"No."

"I wouldn't fret, then. Sound like the smart-ass had it coming, and the other time, you didn't hurt nobody but yourself. It's a bitch growing up poor. The thing is to use your pride rather than letting it light your fuse. When some a-hole says something like that, tell yourself you're already better than him. Just work hard and keep moving ahead, and someday you'll come back to your class reunion driving a Caddy, with a pretty girl beside you, and all the small-town jerks will see what's what. That's the best revenge."

As he sat there in a town he'd never been to before, in the function room of an organization he barely knew existed, at a table with a man he met only a few minutes before, a strange realization came to him.

It felt good, getting advice from Fortin. From his father.

CHAPTER 22

IT WAS PAST seven, and he'd missed the last bus out of town, so he walked back to the highway through a night that hinted winter in the wind and stuck out his thumb. Even in Maine, where the prospect of random violence seemed exceedingly remote, hitchhiking wasn't common anymore. But it was the only option he had.

Surprisingly, his first ride came fast, and he settled back into the seat of a Toyota SUV driven by a muscular ex-military guy in his early forties who wore a pistol on his belt and whose demeanor said don't even dream of messing with me.

That ride took him as far as Bangor, where after half an hour, an older man in a rattletrap pickup gave him a lift that took him past Ellsworth and about five miles down Route 182, toward the Cherryfield woods.

But by then it was late, and traffic was scarce. He'd made a mistake not getting out back on more heavily traveled Route 1, when the man had told him he was turning off "a little shy of Franklin," a town he'd thought was farther along.

The wind was cold now, and penetrating, and he got a flannel shirt out of his pack and put it on over his river driver's pullover, then rolled his jacket collar up and zipped it high up on his chin. Hands jammed in his pockets, he trudged along by moonlight that filtered through the tops of the empty maples. The few cars that traveled the remote road were almost abreast before the drivers noticed him, something he could tell by their belated swerve out across the centerline, and none indicated by so much as a touch of the brakes that they had even considered stopping.

After a while, no one came by at all, and he turned and settled into the rhythm of the walk. He passed the sandy, silvered edge of a large pond whose shore was unmarked by cottages or docks or any other sign of human use.

Off in the forest on its far shore, there came a long, high canid howl, and then, moments after it stopped, an answering ululation from the woods ahead to his right. Wolves. No, it couldn't be. There were none in Maine; they'd been hunted down and eradicated by the early years of the twentieth century, he'd read somewhere. In the *Bangor Daily News*, in a story about the controversy kicked up by a possible plan to reintroduce them into the state's northern woods.

So if not wolves, it had to be coyotes.

Coyotes weren't usually dangerous to people. Ordinarily, you could scare them off with a shout or a clap of the hand or a sudden movement. He thought of Fortin's dog, how it had fought fear to creep toward the roast beef, only to skitter away in alarm when he'd raised his hand up to shoulder level. *Maybe he was part coyote,* he said to himself, and smiled.

The first howl came again, and then the answer, both significantly closer now. He stooped down on the road's shoulder, peering and feeling until he had found four rocks of decent heft, rocks that felt comfortable in his throwing hand. He stuffed them in his jeans' pockets, where they pressed like cold lumps against his leg.

Being alone on the wooded road made him think of the odd psychological quiz Kathy Clarvis had learned somewhere, a set of questions that seemed innocent enough but elicited answers that supposedly revealed your innermost attitudes.

One was to name your favorite animal and explain your choice. After everyone's answers were written down, Kathy said your explanation revealed what you secretly thought of yourself. At that, Gina Robertson, who lived on tony Redoubt Hill, began blushing. Kathy read her answer. She had chosen a cat because they were "beautiful, intelligent, and disdainful."

Another question was how do you feel about being alone in the woods at night? The others had said scared or anxious or uneasy. Not him. *Excited about the adventure of it,* he'd written, with only a little exaggeration.

"That's how you'll face death and the afterlife," Kathy had declared.

His answer had underscored how unlike his classmates he was. He felt that difference now as he walked along the banks of a small lake turned a faint silver by the weak moonlight. But maybe not as different as he had feared. Maybe there wasn't a vicious mole in his nature, a savage, ungovernable side to his psyche.

He thought again of Susan, of what had happened between them that afternoon in the family room of her house when her parents were away. So much worry, fear, obsession, all over nothing, really. A guy sees a nearly naked girl and gets a little carried away. Guys. Most any guy.

And "a little" was right. What, really, had he done? Followed her to the bedroom, hoping for more, and pushed a little too far. But as soon as she had said no—had really said no—he had stopped.

Almost as soon. It hadn't been anything more, really, than the forced kiss you saw in so many old movies, except it hadn't shifted into shared passion the way those always did.

Once back home, he had retrieved the copies he'd made of the newspaper coverage of Fortin's trial from the manila envelope he had carefully duct-taped to the back of his dresser and reread the stories.

> When Davies asked how she could have been raped without bruising or other marking of some sort—the prosecution has acknowledged there was no evidence of physical injury—the girl said that after Fortin had pulled out a knife, she had ceased any attempts to struggle because she feared for her life.

A few paragraphs in particular stood out:

> During his questioning of Moats, Fortin's fellow sailor and friend, Davies asked if he had ever known Fortin to carry a knife, or indeed, even seen him with one.

"I mean, maybe on KP, but not other than that," he said, using the military term for Kitchen Patrol.

Two Lubec police officers who had searched the scene of the alleged rape said they had not found a knife. A Navy investigator who had gone through Fortin's personal gear after his arrest also acknowledged she had not found a knife.

Davies also called to the stand Dr. Elise Crane, a physician at Down East Community Hospital in Machias, who treated the girl the morning after the rape. Under Davies' pointed questioning, she said she hadn't noticed any marks on the girl's neck that would have indicated a sharp object had been pressed against it.

So if it *had* been a rape, it had been a rape with no struggle, no bruising. No struggle, she'd said, because he had had a knife.

But there was no knife, and Fortin's friend said he'd never seen him with one. You couldn't misremember a knife. If there wasn't one, then she'd lied. There was no way around that.

But if he had really held one to her throat, there would have been something. A cut, a prick, a mark, a chafing, a bruise. Wouldn't there?

And didn't the lack of any such evidence point to the conclusion that, at the very least, she had exaggerated what had happened?

Maybe she hadn't really wanted to have sex, but she hadn't made that obvious to him, and so later, she'd felt like it was okay to embellish her account, to add a detail that explained why she hadn't spoken up more forcefully.

But if that was what really happened, wasn't Fortin right that it really hadn't been rape at all? At least, not what most people thought about when they heard the term. Not the kind of thing that should send someone to prison for nine years.

Back at the Center, he watched the other detainees. Some, he was sure, were well on their way to becoming career criminals. He could see it in their baleful gazes, the grim and humorless way they carried themselves, the scorn they had for the rules, the contempt conveyed by their perpetual slouching. In the snippets of conversation he overheard, it was clear some were making their second or third tour of the Center, without ever having contemplated changing course.

Not him. No, not him. He might have lost control of his temper and landed there, but he hadn't lost control of his life, his destiny.

If he could just keep his anger in check, he *wouldn't* be like them.

Then one day, after a session with Dr. Pratt and the later mulling over of his situation it always prompted, it struck him that once he got out, he wouldn't just be freer than the other residents to chart his own course. He would even be freer than his Eastport classmates. They might look at their fathers or mothers and say, *This is what my parents are—this sets the limit for what I can be.*

But his father's chances had been hobbled not just by a long sentence in a real prison but also by the lasting stigma of a rape conviction, which had left him struggling against limited prospects in remote rural Maine.

Before that, before his mother's story—a story he had now come to conclude was fabricated—Lester Fortin had been something different: a small-town kid who had dared to leave home, who was making his way in the world.

Who knew what he might have done if he'd never met Clara Winters?

PART II

CHAPTER 23

GRIFF STEADIED HIS hand and squeezed. Fifty feet away, the wine jug exploded in a shower of green shards. Odd, the way glass broke. Not just splitting along the fracture line where the bullet hit, but disintegrating into dozens of pieces, as if the bullet had destroyed something larger that held it all together.

He'd come every week or so to the gravel pit and practiced, and it was paying off in a growing mastery of the pistol. He had learned its secrets well enough that he could fire six shots in quick succession and regularly see four or five or even all six in the row of jugs shatter.

And yet there was something about the gun that still spooked him, a latent violence in its compact mass that was strange to contemplate. You could own it for months, for years, without anything happening. Then one day, you could aim and shoot, and everything would change, except the gun itself.

And all because of a light squeeze with your index finger, the kind of movement you could make reflexively or in your sleep.

He'd been surprised at how easy it had been to get a handgun. He'd expected the squat, bearded man sitting behind the table at the gun show to ask for his license, to tell him seventeen wasn't old enough, that he needed his father's permission. But he'd merely looked from under hooded eyes as Griff inspected the gun.

"That's a good 'un. But it's got a kick."

He'd handed over four crisp hundreds he'd gotten from the bank, whereupon the man had reached into the pocket of his camouflage jacket and pulled out two twenties and a ten.

"You know how to shoot?"

"Not really."

"Head out to the Rod and Gun Club any Saturday and ask for Lenny. He'll show you."

Instead, he'd gone to the old gravel pit near Round Pond. He'd set some jug wine bottles along a plank, marked twenty paces, flipped the safety off, squinted along the muzzle, and pulled the trigger.

The gun flew back, the heel of his thumb and the edge of the grip striking him on the forehead.

"God-fucking-damn."

He put the pistol down and rubbed at the welt that was already forming. His fingers came away red and wet, and he pulled his T-shirt off and daubed at the cut. Once the bleeding stopped, he took the gun again, and holding it with two hands and tense arms this time, pointed at a bottle and fired.

A balloon-sized cloud of dust rose in the side of the gravel pit. Shot by shot, he emptied the magazine, without hitting anything. He reloaded and moved closer, but even at half the distance, it took four shots before the middle bottle finally shattered.

He was at the Rod and Gun Club at ten a.m. the following Saturday.

An older man with an orange bill cap looked up from the *Bangor Daily News* as he walked in.

"Could someone here show me how to shoot a pistol?"

"Go find Lenny."

"Where's he at?"

"Saddle up and ride to the sound of gunfire." The man guffawed as though he'd said something truly witty, then motioned vaguely toward the back of the building. "He's down at the range. Orange vest, red shirt."

Lenny was a swarthy man with black hair greased back on his head. He took the pistol in his hand and lowered his arm from the elbow, like a lever.

"You got yourself a nice piece here. So what kind of shooting you aiming to do?"

"What kind?"

"What's it for?"

"Just in case I ever need to scare somebody off, like a burglar or something. But I'd never actually shoot at anyone."

"So it's not for shooting?"

"Not really."

"Well, hell, you'd better file the sight off, then."

"Why's that?"

"So it won't hurt so much when somebody takes it from you and shoves it up your ass."

His eyes held Griff's.

"You get what I'm saying?"

"Not really."

"First rule of guns: If you're gonna have one, you gotta be ready to use it. Otherwise, it doesn't do a damn bit of good. And it might just cause you some real harm."

Three sessions with Lenny and he had the basic hang of it. Strong stance, high grasp, hard grip, front sight, smooth pull.

Then he'd practiced until he could stand fifty feet away, bring his right arm smoothly into the brace of his left, and squeeze the trigger just as sights and target came into line. He developed a mnemonic to help ingrain the fluid flow of motion in muscle memory.

Support. Sight. Squeeze.

Support. Sight. Squeeze.

"You secretive son of a bitch. So you took my advice after all," Sonny Beal said the first time he brought him to the gravel pit.

"I was going to get it anyway."

"The fuck you were. So, you any good with it?"

Griff set up a half-dozen wine bottles and fired six quick shots. His friend whistled.

"Goddamn. Question answered. That would transform a certain son of a bitch from crazy to dead in short order."

Griff leveled the gun again, sighted it at the empty air.

"Yeah."

"Show me how."

So he'd demonstrated how to stand like a boxer, not a duelist, how to point the pistol and brace, how the trick was not to hesitate once you had the sights aligned but to squeeze the shot off before your hand started to tremble with the weight.

"It's all kind of one fluid motion."

He handed the pistol over. After three or four shots, one of the bottles exploded. Sonny shot again, and another bottle disappeared in a glitter of glass.

"Goddamn, that's something. I gotta get one. What'd you pay for it?"

"Three-fifty."

"Jesus. That's a lot. But the old man's always saying if I do the traps on the weekends, he'll give me half of what we make those days."

"By yourself?"

"Yeah. He's usually pretty wrecked Saturday and Sunday mornings. But he wants them checked. He says if you don't pull them pretty regular, somebody else will."

"Kinda dangerous, isn't it?"

Sonny shrugged.

"So they say. But lots of fishermen do."

"And some of them end up dead."

"There is that."

"You like lobster?"

"I'm sick of it. He's always sneaking the shorts."

"I guess you'd kick Kate Upton out of bed for snoring."

"She doesn't snore. Or maybe I just get to sleep first. Aaahh— aaaahhh—aaaaahhhhhhhhh—zzzzzzz."

They laughed at the well-worn joke.

"You know what my old man says?"

"What?"

"Used to be so many lobsters you could walk the beach and fill a bucket. Free for the taking. That's what they used to feed the prisoners down at Thomaston. They got so sick of it, they had a riot."

"Guess you would have joined the riot. 'Hey hey, ho ho, nightly lobster's gotta go.'"

"I bet they're not feeding Winters lobster."

"No."

"You think he's coming back?"

"I guess."

"Would you come back to that little shack? And that crazy tub of lard?"

"Not if I had someplace else to go. But he probably doesn't."

They fell silent for a minute.

Beal lined up the last of the bottles and stepped away, and with three quick shots, Griff dispatched them.

"You know, he comes after you, it'd be self-defense, clean and simple. No one in the world would blame you. Not after what he did."

CHAPTER 24

GRIFF FELT BETTER just having the holstered pistol tucked under the truck seat. It restored some peace of mind, something he'd been missing ever since the fight.

"It's not that I'm scared of him," he'd told Sonny. "It's just that he's completely fucking crazy."

What he'd really meant was that he was scared of Winters precisely *because* he was completely fucking crazy. Griff still woke up in a cold sweat some nights, heart thudding, afraid to shut his eyes lest he reenter a nightmare in which Winters, bulked up from a year in reform school, was chasing after him with a club. In the dream, he was running through sand that gave way beneath his feet, while every second, his pursuer gained ground.

"He knocked the wind out of me, so I couldn't fight back," he'd told people in the weeks after the beating, when he was so bandaged and battered that the subject couldn't be avoided.

That was true, in a way. There were those agonizing seconds when he'd gasped for breath, almost paralyzed.

Any normal person would have known that was enough. But Winters had just kept coming, in an explosion of violence unlike anything he'd ever imagined. Down deep, Griff doubted he would have been able to defend himself against that unchecked fury even if he hadn't been sucking for air. You couldn't win a fight with someone that crazy, not unless you were just as crazy yourself.

He could still hear Winters' voice hissing in his ear, just before his head hit the ground for the final time.

"If you ever say anything like that again, I swear, I'll kill you. I will kill you. And if you ever tell a single fucking person, I will kill you. One single person. You understand?"

He'd said he wouldn't, and he'd meant it. He'd even told Sonny to shut his mouth.

"Look, the guy's looney tunes. We don't want to set him off. And besides, if it was you, would you want it getting around? Maybe we owe him that."

"We don't owe him a fucking thing."

"Then do it for me, okay?"

There, he was playing on something unspoken and uneasy between the two of them.

Sonny hadn't egged him on—not exactly—but they both knew it wouldn't have happened if he hadn't been there, making rape gibes under his breath.

"Okay."

CHAPTER 25

"YOU KNOW THIS wouldn't have happened if you weren't friends with Sonny Beal."

Lying in the hospital bed, he looked up at his father through a haze of painkillers.

"It's not his fault."

"I just don't believe that. You never got in fights before you started palling around with him. And Bobby never did. Now look at you, Griff."

"Whatever."

He tried to recall the back-and-forth between the three of them that had left him with the sudden impulse to yell at Winters, but the details wouldn't come through the fog of medication. And anyway, how could you tell what the real impetus was behind something that starts as a snide joke among friends and then suddenly comes out of your mouth as a taunt no one dared you to make but which you'd never have uttered if alone?

"Griffin, you need to listen to your father."

"Mom, my head hurts so bad I can't even think."

Closing his eyes, he feigned falling back to sleep.

"Well, as soon as you feel better, we need to discuss this."

His poor mother, who thought that anything and everything could be solved by an earnest discussion. It would all come back to the same question he had faced since sophomore year: Why did he hang around with Sonny?

The answer, he would decide later, was that Sonny had valued his friendship when no one else did. Early in the fall of that school year, he had taken a random seat in study hall and found himself across from a wiry, dark-haired kid reading a detective novel secreted inside his biology text.

"I'd take the one behind me." A chipped front tooth showed when he spoke.

"Why?"

"Better view. A little hottie with great legs usually sits in that row."

So he had moved—and later, when Jenna Doherty came in barely ahead of the bell and slid into the indicated seat, he'd been glad he had.

"You're the guy who was taking pictures on the breakwater a couple of days ago."

"Yeah."

"You trying to sell 'em?"

"Not really."

"So what's the point?"

"Just trying to get the first light over Campobello. Where were you?"

"On my old man's boat."

"That's early."

"You're telling me."

"You like it?"

"It sucks."

"So why do you do it?"

"He wants help with the traps."

"He could get a partner. Lots of lobstermen do."

"You don't know my old man."

Two weeks had gone by before they had exchanged even the barest of particulars.

"You're Bub, right?"

"Uh-uh. Griff."

"So Bub's your nickname?"

"No. Just Griff."

"Huh. Well, anyways, I'm Sonny. Which kind of sucks, but it's better'n Malcolm, which is my real name."

He and his father and his father's girlfriend had recently moved from Jonesport, Sonny disclosed. His father had heard the lobstering was better here and that there were fewer boats going out.

"When do you see your mom?"

"I don't much. But I'm going back for a few days when school's done."

Sometimes Sonny would sleep the entire period, snoring ever so slightly.

"The old man had me out early," he'd say as he put his head down on his desk. "Wake me up when the bell rings, okay?"

Other times, he'd be jittery on coffee and sit bouncing his feet, ready to tell a dirty joke or pass along a bit of high-school gossip or relate the details of an article he'd read on a website devoted to real-life detective work. There was an arresting knowingness to his acid judgments about teachers and townsfolk, so much so that Griff found himself imitating his cynical style. Which might have been why his parents had grown increasingly inquisitive.

"I'd like you to bring this new friend of yours by the house so we can meet him," his mother said one Saturday as he sat at the kitchen table eating lunch.

"News bulletin: I'm in high school now. Which means I'm old enough to choose my own friends."

"I hear he smokes."

It was true that when he and Sonny walked downtown after school, the first thing Beal did upon leaving school grounds was light a cigarette.

"Granddad smoked, didn't he?"

"And look what it did to him."

"Don't worry, I'm not going to start."

"That's not the point, Griff."

"Then what is?"

"He doesn't seem like your type. You're somebody."

"Bobby is somebody. Not me."

She put a plate in the dishwasher and turned to face him.

"You're going to be somebody too. We expect it of you."

"Yeah, well, you may be disappointed." He'd looked down at the photography magazine, slowly turning a page in a show of indifference.

"And why is that?"

"Because I'm not like Bobby. I'm never going to be a big basketball star or get chosen for the Model UN or be prom king or any of that sh—stuff. I'm just an average guy, and that's okay with me."

"You're not average, Griff, and you shouldn't aspire to that."

"Why not? This town is full of average people, and I'm gonna be one of them."

"I'm *going* to be one of them."

"I thought you didn't like average."

"Don't be flip, Griff. You don't have to be like Bobby. You just need to do your best at something, to stand out in some way."

"Like Dad has done?"

"And just what does that mean?"

"It means, why do you two have such high standards for everybody else? It's not like he's a doctor or a lawyer or anything."

"What he is, Griff, is a businessman who everyone respects and wants to deal with."

"Has to deal with, more like, if they want any heat in the winter. And it's not like he even started the business himself."

His mother was standing across the table from him now, hands on her hips.

"What has gotten into you lately? There are other places to get heating oil. And you should know that the business is twice as large now as it was when your Grandfather Kimball retired."

"Big deal."

"I thought you wanted to work there someday, but I must have misunderstood you. Your father will be disappointed to hear this."

How he loathed her at that moment.

"That wasn't what I meant. I just don't see why it matters that I hang out with somebody whose family doesn't have as much money as we do."

He had expected that to put her on the defensive, but it hadn't.

"His father makes a decent living. Too decent a one, to hear some people tell it."

"What's that supposed to mean?"

She was wiping dishes now and didn't reply. Perhaps she hadn't heard him.

He almost asked again but decided against it. Having battled his way back to even, it was best to leave well enough alone.

One of the things he liked about Sonny was that he considered basketball, the town's civic religion, tedious beyond words.

"I'd rather stick my dick in a can of spiders," he said one day when Griff asked if he was going to the game that Friday.

Griff snorted so hard that heads turned several rows away.

"Why's that?"

"Because basketball bores the hell out of me. But I probably shouldn't say that to the brother of the town's big hero."

"Actually, I get sick of it too."

"Aren't you on the scrub team?"

"JV. My folks made me."

Sonny shook his head in disgust.

"It's pathetic, these little towns. It's all they can talk about. Jonesport's the same way. The Royals, blah blah blah, the tournament, blah blah blah, the refs, blah blah blah."

Suddenly Griff felt defensive.

"What, it's something to go to, anyway. What do you do instead?"

"Come over some night and I'll show you. And bring your camera. You'll be glad you did."

With that, Sonny turned back to the pulp novel he had tucked inside his history book.

It was liberating to find someone who had nothing but disdain for the sport, someone who wasn't always trying to steer the conversation around to Bobby.

Bobby, for whom a first name alone sufficed in Eastport conversation. Bobby, who could go from dribble to jump shot so fast he seemed like a drop of quicksilver on the court. Bobby, who had started for the varsity as a sophomore. Bobby, who, that year, had led an otherwise overmatched team all the way to the state championship game before a taller Upper Kennebec Valley squad had squeezed out a victory in a contest so close it wasn't decided until the final moments.

He was sick to death of being asked about Bobby—of being expected to know how many points his brother had gotten in this game or that. The truth was, Bobby was a scoring machine, someone who always wanted the ball in those crucial seconds when games are won or lost.

He himself hated those make-or-break moments. For him, the risk of a mistake always loomed larger than the chance for glory. In one tight home game, with Washington Academy's JV squad pressing hard, he had run to his assigned spot near center court when a hard pass had come from Kenny Cook, the Tigers' double-teamed guard. He hadn't expected the ball—Cook, an adroit dribbler, usually brought it up himself—and the high pass ricocheted off his sweaty hands.

He had turned downcourt, but it wasn't there. But where?

Just as he had completed a full frantic pivot, the ball, which had been deflected straight up, bounced on the top of his head. As a roar of laughter rose from the crowd, a nearby Washington Academy player retrieved it and raced downcourt for a breakaway layup.

Red-faced and mortified, he had been relieved when the exasperated Tigers coach had signaled for a substitution, and he sunk gladly into the anonymity of the bench.

He had tried and tried to learn the mechanics of Bobby's lightning jump shot. At their mother's behest, his brother had spent an hour or so every week critiquing his progress and demonstrating, again and again, the transition from dribble to shot, the quick jump at the start, the wrist flick and follow through at the finish.

"So it's Up, Hang, Bang, Come Down. Up, Hang, Bang, Come

Down."

Like you have a choice about coming down, he wanted to say as his brother repeated the mantra for the nth time.

Instead, he tried to mimic the move, to make it his own. But pulling up so quickly threw his dribble off, and that ruined his timing.

"Let's call it quits for the day."

Bobby took the ball from him. "Try it this way. Three dribbles, then stop right here. Then: Up, Hang, Bang, Come Down."

His quick shot sent the ball snapping through the chain net. He retrieved it, dribbled out to the top of the key, and took another shot. Again, the ball arced through the hoop, hitting nothing but chain.

"So, same routine each time. Start here. Dribble, dribble, dribble, shoot. Dribble, dribble, dribble, shoot."

He threw Griff the ball.

"I've had enough. Let's knock off."

"Not yet. Do it ten times, then we'll go. Muscle memory."

"Tomorrow."

"You've got to keep at it if you want to get better."

"I know, I know. But I've got other stuff I want to do today."

"You think I don't? There's a party at the lake."

"So go. It's not like I want every Saturday to be basketball camp."

"You gotta keep practicing if you want to get better, sport."

"It's Griff."

"Touchy, touchy."

"Because I like to be called by my name?"

"Sport's what Dad calls you."

"Yeah, well, you're my brother, not my father. In case you hadn't noticed."

Bobby stared at him, eyes narrowing.

"Whatever you say, Bub."

Griff opened his mouth to reply, but the words were welling up inside him, jamming against one another in an angry rush to get out.

"Fu . . . fu . . . fu . . ."

Bobby walked over to where he had left his sweatshirt, then turned and looked back, the left corner of his mouth arching disdainfully.

"That's the stuff, Bub."

Pivoting sideways, Griff whipped the ball as hard as he could at his brother. His verbal logjam broken by the hard physical motion, the words came racing out.

"Fuck you, Bobby." His brother ducked, but not fast enough. The ball grazed the top of his head. "Fuck you. Fuck you. Fuck you."

Bobby was reaching for a rock now, and Griff turned and sprinted away, tears of rage running down his cheeks.

CHAPTER 26

ONE THURSDAY WHEN Griff's parents were away in Bangor, he decided to take Sonny up on his cryptic invitation.

"Come around eight-thirty. And don't forget your camera."

Sonny's father and his girlfriend were watching TV in the living room, but his friend led him upstairs without introduction. Once in his room, Sonny sat on the sloppily made bed and gestured toward the chair.

"Want a beer?"

"You've got some?"

"Home brew. The old man makes it."

"He lets you drink it?"

"Let's just say he's not good at inventory control."

Sonny dropped to his knees, reached under the bed, and pulled out a plastic bucket that held six dark bottles nestled in ice. He took an opener from his pocket, pried the cap off one, and handed it to Griff.

"Drink it easy. If you tilt it too far back, you'll get the sludge from the bottom, and it tastes like shit."

Griff took a mouthful and swallowed. It was tingly and sweet, almost like the champagne he had sipped at a New Year's Eve party. He took another gulp.

"It takes some getting used to. But finish that bottle and you'll be feeling no pain."

"They don't notice you taking it?"

"Not as long as I don't get greedy. He makes a lot, and he and Slut Butt both hit it pretty hard."

"Slut Butt?"

"That's what my mom calls her. She stole him away. Not that he's any prize."

"What if they come in?"

"Why would they?"

"Maybe to see if we're drinking their beer." He guffawed.

"Told you it's got a kick." Sonny reached into his shirt pocket, took out a pack of Marlboros, and lit one.

"Your dad doesn't care if you smoke?"

"Why, when it means he's got someone to bum 'em from?" He tilted the pack toward Griff. "Want one?"

"Nope. My grandfather died of lung cancer."

Sonny shrugged.

"The old man always says that if you're a lobsterman, something else'll kill you before cancer gets around to it."

"You're going to be a lobsterman?"

"No. I'm gonna get out of this goddamn town and out of this goddamn state as soon as I can. But I still think something'll get me before cancer does."

Griff took another swallow.

"I like this town."

"Which is your constitutional right."

"So what's wrong with it?"

"Nothing, unless you want to live someplace where they don't roll the sidewalks up at night."

"Like . . . ?"

"Miami."

"And do what?"

"Be a private eye. With a speedboat and a Jag."

"I thought detectives had to blend in."

"Not if you know what you're doing."

"Like you do."

"I guarantee I know a fuck of a lot more about what's going on in this town than you. And you've lived here your whole life."

"So tell me something I don't know."

Sonny tilted his head back as though selecting from a large mental inventory.

"Let's see. You know why Sloggy Jefferson's pickup is parked in the North End every Friday and Saturday night?"

Griff rolled his eyes.

"I guess I should have been more specific. I meant, tell me something I don't know that I might actually want to know. The whereabouts of Sloggy's pickup doesn't qualify."

He thought of their high-school history teacher, in his habitual uniform of dark slacks, blue or white button-down shirt, and corduroy sports coat with leather elbow patches. Since his divorce, Jefferson had been huffing and puffing through town on a regular jog, one whose slow pace had earned him his nickname.

"Have it your way then." Sonny smiled knowingly, but Griff refused to bite.

They sat there for a minute, and then Sonny reached for the bucket and pulled a second bottle of home brew out of the ice.

"Want another?"

"Yeah."

He lifted his bottle to his mouth and tried to finish it in one long pull.

"Phhlaaaah." Reaching for the mug Sonny was using for an ashtray, he spat out the gritty dregs.

"Told ya." Sonny laughed as Griff sloshed some beer from the new bottle around his mouth and then spat it, too, into the mug.

"Hey, why do some kids call you Bub?"

"They fucking don't."

His vehemence surprised him.

"A few do. I've heard 'em."

"A few assholes."

"But why?"

"Some bullshit thing a couple of morons came up with in grammar school to bug me."

Griff tried to change the subject, but Sonny wasn't ready to move on.

"Know how to make 'em stop?" He stood up and made a sudden thrust with his knee. "The next guy who says it, let him have it right in the balls. That'll end it. Guaranteed."

Shortly after ten p.m., Sonny went to the desk, pulled out two pairs of yellow marine binoculars, and handed him one.

"Get your camera ready." He opened the last two beers, handed one to Griff, and raised his own.

"To American girls."

"American girls."

They clinked the long necks and drank.

"Okay, train your binocs that way." Sonny gestured to the left.

"All I see is a tree branch."

Sonny flipped the light off and pushed up the window. He reached out and pulled a length of thick monofilament fishing line into the room. There was a loop on the end. Fighting the obvious tension of the line, he slipped it over a nail driven into the baseboard.

"And now, thanks to the wonders of pulleys and some kick-ass engineering, that tree branch has relocated itself. So what do you see now?"

"A window."

"That's the stage for tonight's miracles. And . . . it's . . . showtime."

A figure appeared in the lighted window. A girl in profile, running her hands through her hair. With one fluid motion, she crossed her arms and pulled off her T-shirt. She stood still for a moment in jeans and a pale blue bra, looking into a mirror.

"May I present Miss Megan Hall, starring in 'Let's Choose Tomorrow's Outfit.'"

Megan was a high-school cheerleader, a senior he frequently saw at the center of a laughing flock of older girls.

Now she eased a flowered peasant blouse on, appraised herself for thirty seconds or so, then took it off again. She slipped her bra straps down her shoulders, pulled the clasp around and unfastened it, and set it behind her, affording him a brief, tantalizing view of her bare breasts. As she turned back, she glanced their way, and her eyes seemed to meet his.

Griff ducked.

"Fuck, I think she saw me."

"Relax. It's the binocs. Her light is on, ours is off, so she can't see anything. Besides, she's used to the branch being there."

When Griff raised the binoculars again, the girl had turned back to the mirror. She reached behind her and pulled the same blouse back on, then looked again.

"Think she's done it yet?"

"The wild thing?" Sonny shook his head. "If she had, she wouldn't act so dreamy. Sometimes she leans forward and starts kissing the mirror."

"I'd love to see that."

"Beggars can't be choosers."

"More like, voyeurs can't be choosers."

"What the fuck is a voyeur?"

"Umm, you are. A peeping Tom."

"I don't see your eyes closed."

"Does she do this every night?"

"Just about."

"God, you're lucky."

"Luck's got nothing to do with it. It's the payoff for careful surveillance. And some pretty good work in the tree."

Now the girl disappeared from view.

"Can you take her in this light?"

"Maybe. With a long exposure."

"Then get ready. The best is about to come."

A moment later, she was back. She unbuttoned her jeans and, with a wiggle or two, slid them off her legs.

"Better have another swallow. Your heart's gonna need it."

They each drank. She started brushing her hair. Her breasts rose and fell with the motion of her arm.

"She doesn't stop until she's done a hundred strokes. Me, I'm usually done in half that."

"This is fucking amazing."

"So take some pictures."

"Her arm will be blurry."

"Dude, who gives a rat's ass about her arms?"

Kneeling by the window, he rested his telephoto lens on the sill, set a long shutter speed, and pressed the delayed release. He didn't want to waste timing checking the images, so after two or three clicks, he changed the exposure. Finally, she stopped brushing and ran her fingers through hair, raising it up and letting it cascade onto the top of her breasts.

"God."

". . . is great."

Sonny pushed the window back down.

"Show's over. Now she hops into bed and dreams of the day when she won't be alone there." He pointed to the camera. "Let's see what you got."

"Not now. I've got to get home before my folks or I'm screwed."

He broke into a run as soon as he hit the end of Sonny's gravel sidewalk. The beer sloshed heavily in his gut as he loped along the dark streets. His ears were pounding, and he was sucking wind by the time he rounded the corner onto his street.

No Prius. Just his father's pickup in the driveway. He let himself in the unlocked kitchen door.

When his mother woke him the next morning, his head was thudding, and his stomach roiled with nausea so near it made his jaw tremble. He stood in the shower and let the hot water pound down on him, feeling physically and mentally sketchy.

It wasn't until school got out that he had a chance to look at the photos. The girl's arms were a study in fluid motion, but her breasts were in sharp focus in some of the shots. She was lithe and lovely there in the window, framed in a glow that was almost magical.

Scrolling through them, he felt an odd swirl of pride and guilt. They had an ethereal look of the sort you might see in a Portland gallery. They were art, or at least arty, yet they had come from something sleazy enough that he felt ashamed.

Still, he found himself eager for an encore, though he knew his parents would be skeptical of him staying out past ten on a school night.

Which is when he hit upon the inspiration of doing his history project with Sonny. Once a year, Jefferson required teams of two or three to research a topic and then make a twenty-minute presentation. It was a way to fill up class time without actually having to teach, Griff had heard other faculty members grumble. But it was just the excuse he needed.

"We'll do ours together. My folks can't object to me coming over if it's for school."

They had chosen the Lincoln–Douglas debates. The first week, he had taken pains to leave several library books open in the den, after which, at least once a week, he'd announce he was going to Sonny's to work on their history project and would be back by eleven.

They actually did do a little work, scanning through a few of the debates and taking some notes. But before long, Sonny would reach under the bed and bring out whatever home brew he'd been able to stash, and they'd sit and drink and wait for Megan to begin her nightly routine.

He bought a bottle of mint mouthwash, which he kept in Sonny's desk, and before he left, he'd take a swig and swish it around in his mouth as he walked home.

If his parents were up when he came in, they were usually watching TV, which meant he could head to his room to revisit his latest images of Megan.

CHAPTER 27

"IF MY MOM comes in, you'll have ruined the whole point."

"Which is?"

"To show that we actually do some smart things."

They were in Griff's room on a rainy Friday night, playing Scrabble, a game whose principal pleasure for Sonny was forming off-color words. "Tits" and "dicks" were his first two, and he had just played "ass."

Sonny snorted.

"I could walk across the bay, and your old lady would still think I'm a loser. You know why?"

"Umm, because you are?"

He'd expected Sonny's lazy laugh, not the edgy tone of his reply.

"Because I'm not like Bobby's friends. And that means you're not like Bobby."

"Nah. They just want us to be doing worthwhile stuff."

"Face it, Griff. The sun shines out of his butt as far as they're concerned. Big basketball star, good-looking, popular, sure to go to a good college."

He locked his jaw together and tilted his nose up.

"He's such a credit to Eastport."

Then, switching to a deeper but equally plummy tone, he started an imaginary dialogue.

"But what about the younger son, Grit?"

"You must mean Griff."

"Yes, yes, Griff. What's the story with him?"

"I hear he hangs out with that Beal boy."

"Oh my. A regular juvenile delinquent, that one. Why, he doesn't even play basketball."

"Worse yet, I hear he smokes. And they drink. Neither one will amount to anything."

"It must be so hard for poor Carlton and Estelle to bear."

"Estelle and Carlton. She wears the pants in that family."

Griff got up from his chair.

"Fuck you, Sonny."

"And did I mention they occasionally employ profanity in their conversation?"

"Knock it off."

"Just telling it like it is."

There was, he had to admit, an uncomfortable truth to Sonny's commentary.

Although they made a regular effort to draw him out about his doings, his parents' world revolved around Bobby. He'd respond to their queries with a banality or two about his classes, then wait for the conversation to follow its natural course back to Bobby and last week's triumphs or Bobby and the upcoming game with Calais or Woodland or Sumner or Narraguagus. Or Bobby and his application to the Naval Academy and the choice he might have to make between a free ride there and the pricier prospect of acceptance at Bowdoin or Dartmouth or Middlebury.

They didn't inquire about Griff's own post-high-school hopes in dinner-table conversations. Maybe they thought it was too early to push, but more likely, they knew his modest goals would pale alongside Bobby's.

Bobby, after all, had plans to travel the world, once he finished at the Naval Academy or Bowdoin or wherever. And then to go to law school and rise up through the JAG ranks or move to Portland or Boston or Washington DC.

"I want to go somewhere big and make it there," Bobby said on one such occasion.

"On the other hand, if you stay in Maine, you could run for office," his mother said. "Someday you could be governor, or maybe even a US senator."

"Don't you have to win an election to get those jobs?" Griff had almost interjected.

Of course, even if Bobby chose to grace Maine with his continued presence, the assumption was that he'd live in Portland or Falmouth or Cape Elizabeth, not Eastport or Calais or Machias or even Bangor.

But why did you have to leave? Sometimes, when he drove along the causeway that connected Eastport to the mainland and the sun and tide were both high, leaving the bay brimming with dancing, sparkling seawater, the evergreens lush from the frequent rain, he was convinced there was no more beautiful place on Earth.

Was it so bad to want to stay where you had grown up? That was what the vast majority of people did, after all. Yes, the overachievers might go away to elite schools and move to tony neighborhoods in bustling cities and jet around the globe on business and spend their vacations touring Europe or on safari in Africa, but most people lived their lives where they were raised.

Which was exactly what he wanted to do—work for the family business, find a nice girl, get married, settle down.

Why was that a disappointing path? After all, if everybody had to work on Wall Street or earn their stripes in Washington or Boston or Portland, then little towns like Eastport would just dry up and blow away.

Sonny finally played his word—"prick"—and picked another four tiles.

"I've got a little thing here you could have some fun with."

"Sorry. I'm not gay. But I respect the fact that you are—and that you're open about it."

"Funny, Griff, funny." He reached into his coat and took out a miniature digital recorder.

"It's voice-activated."

"Voice-activated? What's that mean?"

His sarcasm had apparently been too subtle, for Sonny mistook it for a real question.

"It starts recording whenever someone nearby starts talking, then stops when they stop."

Griff transfigured his face into a look of mock amazement.

"Oh my Lord. What will they dream up next, space travel?"

Sonny ignored his mockery, which only made him more determined.

"Or maybe even a miniature clock—one that wouldn't have to be wound—that you can strap to your wrist so you'll always know what time it is."

His friend waited until he had run out of gibes and then got to what had no doubt been his point all along.

"Maybe if you hid it in your brother's car, we could find out how he charms the thongs off so many hotties."

"No f-ing way."

"Why f-ing not?"

"Umm, because if he found out, he'd kill me?"

"How's he gonna find out? Does he check his car every morning for bombs?"

"If people knew what he was really like, he'd sure have to."

"Just do it."

"It probably makes a noise."

"I've been recording us. Have you heard anything?"

Griff shook his head.

"No, but it's still a stupid idea, so drop it."

And Sonny had, at least until he left.

"Hey, don't forget that," Griff said, gesturing toward where it lay on the bed.

"I have another one." He smiled archly. "Do whatever you want with it."

He experimented with the recorder the next day, listening for any sound that might give it away. There was none. The microphone was sensitive enough to pick up his voice all the way across the room. But it wasn't as if you'd hear any conversation over a car stereo, anyway.

He slipped it into his drawer and forgot about it.

Forgot about it until one Friday a few weeks later, when Bobby sought him out in his room.

"Hey, Griff, how ya doin'?"

He looked up from his photography magazine.

"I'm good."

"Hey, think you could do me a favor?"

"What?"

"Just between us, right?"

"Sure."

"Absolutely no word to anyone?"

"Got it, Bobby. What's up?"

"The 'rents are going to St. Stephen's on Friday for some cross-border Rotary thing, and they won't be back till late. And I've got a date with Amy Arden, the new girl who moved here from Portland."

"Lucky you."

"You know her?"

"She's in my algebra class. She's nice."

"A smokeshow. Anyway, I was thinking she and I could have some fun if we had the house to ourselves."

"Sure. I'll hang with Sonny."

"Till eleven-thirty or so?"

"Yeah. I'll call your cell when I'm heading home."

"Thanks, Griff. You're a pal."

His brother flashed his trademark grin. Each time he did, Griff was left wondering if he was whitening his teeth.

"No problem. You like her?"

"I like what I see. And I want to see more."

He had to wait until Bobby had gone out for a run on Saturday morning to retrieve the recorder. Back in his own room, he hit play.

"I like your room."

"I like having you in my room. You want some wine?"

"Sure. Where'd you get it?"

"Up in Robbinston."

"You got a fake ID?"

"Nope."

"So how?"

"Act the part and you'll look the part."

A few seconds passed, then the sound of her giggling.

"It's a good thing you're not a sommelier, Bobby."

"A what?"

"A wine steward."

"Why?"

"It's pretty sweet."

"That's bad?"

"It's not good."

"You know about wine?"

"Some. My folks had a restaurant before . . . before they split up."

"Maybe you could teach me."

"Well, the first thing is . . ."

"But not now."

Some time had apparently elapsed. When the recording started again, it was her voice.

"You're sure your folks won't be back?"

"Positive. And my brother is off with his weird friend."

"Your brother?"

"Griff."

"Stupid me. I hadn't put two and two together."

"We're pretty different."

"How so?" Her voice conveyed genuine curiosity.

"Well, you know. Griff is Griff."

"Which means . . . ?"

"He's got issues."

"Like?"

"Like, he spends most of his time doing his award-winning impression of a bump on a log."

She giggled a little, then affected a scolding tone.

"I can't believe you'd say that about your own brother. He's in algebra with me, and he's really sweet. I'm completely lame at math, and he's so nice about helping me. And he's funny."

"Funny? Griff? Funny like Homer Simpson, you mean."

"No, seriously. Sometimes he makes droll little comments that just crack me up."

"Give me an example."

"I can't, right off the top of my . . . Well, okay, one day in history class, Mr. Jefferson got going on this long spiel about how if there were other beings out there in the universe and they came to Earth, they'd be all peaceful, and did we know why, and no one did. He said it was because if they'd made it to the stage of advanced space travel, they'd have survived their own nuclear era and their own arms race, and *that* meant they'd have realized what insanity it was and so had found a way to get along without war.

"Anyway, he just kept going on and on, and everyone was like 'Oh my God, kill us now and put us out of our misery,' and all of a sudden, Griff hands me this note that says, 'He's certainly explained the Vulcans, but how does he account for the Klingons?' I giggled, and Mr. Jefferson saw I had a note and made me read it in front of the class, and when I did, everybody started laughing, except for the kids who'd never seen the *Star Trek* movies. Then Mr. Jefferson got all mad and said it was too bad, since he was so witty, that Griff never saw fit to participate in class. After that, whenever he'd say something philosophical, he'd add, 'Perhaps that has inspired a witticism that Griff would like to share with us.'"

"The class cracked up over that?"

"It was really funny, in the moment and all. You just don't want to give him any credit. You know, it can't be easy, being your brother."

"Hey, I'm always there for him. But it's like living with a mime."

"He acts everything out?"

"No, I mean, he doesn't talk."

She giggled.

"You mean a mute."

"Whatever. I call him Mr. Mope."

"You're mean," she said, but in a mostly flirtatious tone. "Why do you think he's so quiet when you're so chatty?"

"The 'rents think it comes from stuttering. He used to something wicked, as a kid. 'Bub . . . bub . . . bub . . . bub. The other kids started making fun of him, so then he just clammed up. My folks had to send him someplace in Portland."

"It must have worked. I've never heard him stutter."

"Maybe because he hardly ever says anything."

"He talks to me. Maybe it's you, Bobby."

"Me?"

"You're intimidating. I'm not sure I'd want you as my brother . . ."

"Me neither. Because then this would be wrong."

Next came a few murmurs, and then the recording stopped. It picked up again with his brother's voice.

"That is so damn sexy. Where'd you get it?"

"Victoria's Secret, at the Maine Mall."

"First time I've seen something like that on an actual girl."

"I'm supposed to believe that? A big Romeo like you?"

"Now, let's see, how does it come off?"

"I bet you can figure it out."

When the recording started again, her voice was louder.

"Bobby, please don't."

"We've got the house all to ourselves. Let's have a good time."

"I *was* having a good time."

"Let's have an even better time."

"Is that what you thought when you asked me to hang out?"

"I thought you'd at least make me feel good."

"From what I hear, guys can take care of that by themselves."

"That's not what I had in mind."

"I'm not doing what you have in mind. *Any* of the things you have in mind. Not on a first date."

"So, nothing?"

"If this is nothing, I guess not."

"I'd heard you Portland girls were liberated, but you're just a cock tease."

There was some rustling, a squeak of springs, the sound of feet on the floor.

"Oh come on. Don't go."

"Bye, Bobby. Sorry to be such a disappointment."

Then came Bobby, low and angry, seemingly talking to himself.

"Fucking bitch."

CHAPTER 28

HE LAY ON the floor, fingers interlaced behind his head, forearms pressing hard against his temples, his breath coming in short, agonized gasps.

"You fucking asshole. You no-good fucking asshole."

Let it go. It didn't matter. His brother should be ashamed, not him. Besides, the humiliation he felt made no sense. Without the recorder, he wouldn't have known what Bobby had said. And Bobby and Amy would never know that he knew.

It was like it hadn't even happened.

Plus, Amy liked him and thought he was funny. She had obviously seen through Bobby. Lying there, he vowed he'd never use girls like his asshole brother did, never treat them as just another conquest to notch his belt.

In a way, his secret knowledge gave him an advantage. Still, he wished a life-altering trauma like stuttering would someday afflict his brother.

Like any number of kids, when he was younger, he'd had some trouble differentiating sounds. Sometimes when he tried to form words, it was as though something slipped a cog for a second. It wasn't awful—not at first—just something that happened from time to time. He wasn't even that conscious of it.

Not until that day in sixth grade. They had been studying the New England whaling industry, and Mrs. Sheets, a stern woman with short gray hair, had asked how whalers had obtained whale oil.

No hands went up.

"Can't anyone tell me? You're supposed to have studied this."

The class sat in a silent conspiracy of ignorance.

"Perhaps you can help us, Griffin."

He knew, or at least he thought he did. With sperm whales, it had come from cavities in their heads, but with the others, it was from the fat.

"By boiling the blub . . . bub . . . blub . . ."

He took a breath and tried again.

"The bub . . . blub . . . bub . . ."

He could feel his face turning red, his heartbeat pounding in his throat.

"The blub . . . bub . . . bub . . ."

His mouth had become so dry he couldn't wet his lips. A twitter of amusement was rising in the room, suppressed giggling giving way to open laughs.

Eyes closed in a squint of concentration, he tried again.

"The bub . . . bub . . . bub . . ."

Finally, the word came out, wrong but whole: "bubber."

The entire class was laughing now.

"That's enough," Mrs. Sheets barked. "The next person who makes a noise will spend half an hour with me after school."

The taunt sprang up almost instantly.

"Griffy Kimball has lips of rubber. That's what makes him blub-bub-bubber."

The teachers put a stop to the schoolyard mockery, but that had just driven the derision underground. He would sometimes hear "Hey, Bub!" yelled from around a corner, but most often, he would encounter the mockery scrawled inside school bathroom stalls. He started carrying a magic marker with him to black out the jeer, but it reappeared with the tenacity of bamboo.

A tight ball of terror now rose in his throat whenever he was called on. His heart would start racing before he had even opened his mouth, and after the first few syllables, his tongue would stick and trip, unwilling to move from the first hard consonant to the vowels that followed. Even simple math answers fractured into an infinite string of broken sounds.

And so, he'd sit agonized and stuck, the T or D or B sound echoing endlessly from his mouth, until his face burned red and tears of frustration filled his eyes.

Sympathetic to his plight, teachers had quit calling on him. His self-consciousness grew so acute that he refrained from speaking even on the playground. Because he no longer talked to them, the other kids had stopped talking to him.

And so he had come to inhabit a zone of silence.

It was only away in Portland in residential speech therapy that he had learned to relax himself by imagining his classmates naked or by recalling a favorite joke, to inhale and exhale regularly as he spoke. And, most importantly, to stop when a verbal block was immovable and make light of his stuttering with a guttural sound: "It's a ba . . . ba . . . ba . . . Grrrrr! It's a baboon."

Because he'd missed so much school, he'd had to repeat a grade. Normally, there would have been some shame in staying back, but for him, it had been a relief, a change that helped free him from his humiliations.

Still, as glad as he was to leave his old class, he couldn't help feeling out of place in his new one. Even though speech therapy had let him mostly overcome his problem, it was easier and safer to keep quiet in class. And so, he developed a reputation as reserved and standoffish.

It wasn't that he was disliked—he wasn't, as far as he could tell—but rather that he didn't have close friends. He was a kid the other boys would gladly pick as a fourth or fifth choice in a recess game of kickball or basketball but one they'd never think about calling when they had friends over to play video games.

So he had found other things to do. He had taken up photography and had persuaded his parents to subscribe to Netflix so he could watch the great old films.

When he'd started high school, he'd found there was ample room to be one of the quiet kids who endure rather than thrive. His parents had insisted that he try out for basketball, and he had, but despite being taller than average, he was only a middling player. Part of it—a not-understood, un-coachable aspect—was that he couldn't bring himself to yell for the ball on a fast break or when open underneath.

He wasn't lonely, not really, or at least, not desperately so. The thing that bothered him most was his awkwardness around girls. The only ones he spoke to were those who sat near him in class and sometimes asked for his help. Girls like Amy Arden and Susan Jameison, who would never think of him as a romantic possibility and just as obviously weren't worried about him seeing them that way.

But if it wasn't an awful existence, it was an empty one.

And then one day early in the fall of his sophomore year, the wiry new kid with the chipped front tooth had looked his way in study hall and casually advised him where to sit for the best view of Jenna Doherty's legs.

CHAPTER 29

"CATCH, GRIFF."

With a pitcher's deft reflexes, Griff snagged the small red wad Sonny tossed his way from his bedroom closet. It was a lacy thong.

"Wow. . . It must get cold lobstering in these."

"Funny, dude, funny."

His friend's flat tone tried to convey that he didn't think so, but Griff could sense otherwise. It was the kind of deft quip they prided themselves on.

"So whose are they?"

"They're a clue."

"About you?"

"About Sloggy and why his pickup is parked in the North End so often."

"You mean he's doing it with the owner of these?"

"You're crushing it, Griff. Just crushing it."

Griff gave the thong a closer look. The "Figleaves" label said they were pure silk. He couldn't imagine anyone who would wear them finding Jefferson the least bit attractive.

"So who is she?"

Sonny shook his head in feigned regret.

"I'd like to tell you, but I'm afraid it would break your lonely high-school heart."

"Do I know her?"

"Not the way he does. But you'd give your left nut to."

"C'mon."

Sonny frowned.

"Well, maybe another clue." He gazed at the ceiling for a few seconds and rubbed his chin. "*Parlez-vous français*, Monsieur Kimball?"

"Oh my God, no. Tell me you're kidding."

"Nope. He's banging your beloved French teacher. And what's more, Mademoiselle Laurent likes it on top."

New to Shead High the previous year, Miss Laurent was in her mid-twenties, and with an exotic accent, dark eyes, and dirty-blonde hair cut in a top-of-the-shoulder shag, she was the object of mesmerized awe for most of the high-school males, a role she seemed to find both flattering and amusing.

"You spied on them?"

"It's what detectives do."

Griff snorted.

"More like what peeping Toms do." And then, when Sonny didn't reply: "And she was on top?"

Sonny threw his head back and bit his lower lip, then started rubbing his chest.

"You're kidding."

"With God as my witness."

"You'd better hope he wasn't."

"The Lord would want her perfect beauty enjoyed by all. He had Eve run around naked, after all."

"Was she completely naked?"

"Both her and Adam. Or so the Bible tells us."

"You know what I mean, asshole."

"Not even a nightie to offend God's eye."

"Oh man, I'd love to see that."

Sonny took a pull on his cigarette, tilted his head back, and blew a plume of smoke his way.

"So come with me Saturday. Get her on camera."

"Not my thing."

"Tell that to Megan."

"That's different."

"Why?"

Griff found he couldn't really say. Still, it was one thing to sit in Sonny's room and watch, something very different to sneak up behind somebody's house and spy on them.

"It just is."

"What's different is, here, you don't have to worry about getting caught."

"It'd be just my luck that we would."

Sonny rolled his eyes.

"For fuck's sake, we're not gonna get caught. She rents one of those old places on the other side of the cemetery. You just go through the woods, climb down the slope, and the view is there to enjoy."

"So, just like a national park."

"A national nudist park. And because she likes it on top, you don't have to watch Sloggy's fat butt bouncing up and down."

"Does she give the deep kiss?"

Sonny shook his head.

"Oh no. You want the slime, you gotta do the crime. But you probably shouldn't, the way you worship her, because you'll never look at her the same way again."

A few minutes passed before Griff spoke again.

"What if somebody sees us and calls the cops, and they spot us a few blocks away, at night, with a camera?"

"Spot us? In the woods? Not gonna happen."

"Say it does."

"Then we say we're out looking for a great horned owl. I said there was one on the island, you said no way, so we made a bet."

"What if we've got pictures on the camera?"

"We take the memory card out as soon as we're done and hide it in the woods and come back for it later. Then if anybody stops us, we say we didn't realize it was gone until we tried to take some pictures."

Griff fretted his lips.

"I don't know."

"You are such a pussy. Why don't you just put that on?" He pointed toward the thong, which Griff still had in his hand.

CHAPTER 30

"AFTER THIS ONE."

As soon as the taillights receded, they darted across High Street and ducked into the cemetery. He followed Sonny to the end of the graveyard, where they pulled themselves over the chest-high fence.

"Down this way."

The light woods turned to tall brush, which eventually gave way to rocky outcroppings.

"It's that one over there. And . . . the . . . lights . . . are . . . on."

A dog's frenzied bark sounded somewhere off to their right. They dropped to a crouch.

"Jesus, Sonny."

The dog kept up its barking. After thirty seconds or so, a light appeared in a nearby house, and the back door opened.

"Cappy, stop that."

"We need to get closer," Sonny whispered when the barking had subsided. "There's a big rock we can hide behind down there."

Crouched, they crept along the rocky perimeter until Sonny reached a point opposite the house.

"It gets steep, but there's plenty of stuff to grab onto."

Sonny worked his way nimbly down the short slope and forward until he was behind a sizable boulder, then turned and beckoned.

With the camera hanging from his neck, Griff had to go more carefully. Using a crease in the stone for purchase, he worked his way down. Once at the bottom, he crept to where Sonny crouched.

"They're still eating."

They were both at the table, Sloggy in a blue button-down, Miss Laurent in a scoop-neck blouse, a bottle of wine between them.

"Let's hope they're having oysters."

"Don't make me laugh, dickhead."

They watched for several minutes as the two sat and ate, seemingly without speaking.

Suddenly she put her fork down and said something.

Jefferson set his wineglass on the table and, leaning back in his chair, brought his hands behind his head so his elbows flared to the side. Griff could see his lips move. She stood and left the room.

Now she appeared in the kitchen window. He could see the frown that creased her forehead and the tight line of her lips.

"They're fighting."

"No shit, Sherlock."

Jefferson entered the room. She turned and faced him, waving her arms in an arc that ended in a palms-up gesture. Jefferson took two quick steps forward and shoved his left hand up under her chin, yoking her neck with his thumb and fingers. Keeping her pinned to the wall, he slapped her face, first with his palm and then with his backhand, and then again.

"Jesus Christ. We gotta do something."

"Like what?"

"Yell. Or throw something."

"Then we'd be the ones in deep shit."

Jefferson snarled something at her, slapped her again, then removed his hand from her throat. She crumpled into the corner.

"We should call the police."

"No fucking way. They'd want to know how we knew. And they'd have our number."

"We could say we heard a scream."

"She didn't scream. Let it go. She pissed him off, he taught her a lesson. Happens all the time. I bet your old man has done it once or twice."

"No way."

"Huh."

"I'd know."

Sonny snorted.

"Okay, Griff. It happens all the time, just never with *your* folks."

He could feel anger building up in him now—anger at what he'd seen, anger at his own impotence, anger at Sonny and his insinuations.

"You got a knife?"

"Yeah. Why?"

"I've fucking had it with assholes. I'm gonna teach that motherfucker a lesson."

"You're going after him with a knife? Are you outta your fucking mind?"

"Not him. His truck."

"Not worth the trouble, Griff. Let's go."

"Give me the knife."

"Have it your way."

Sonny reached in his pocket and brought out a jackknife.

"Where's he parked?"

"Up the block."

They sneaked along the side of the house to the street.

"Right there." Sonny gestured. "As though no one can guess where he is."

Crouching by the pickup's right front tire, Griff pushed the blade against the sidewall and began turning it.

"It's a knife, not a fucking drill. Slash it."

Griff sliced at the rubber until he heard the sibilant hiss of escaping air.

A door slammed.

"Shit, it's him. Let's go."

They scrambled away from the truck and lay in the tall grass of the roadside gully.

Swearing under his breath, Jefferson climbed into the cab, started the engine, and revved it hard. Gravel came spitting back, peppering them with stinging bits of stone.

Griff stuck his head up enough so that he could see the truck as it accelerated down the hill. Suddenly, it fishtailed, then spun out of control and slammed into a fire hydrant. Water began shooting from under its bonnet.

"Oh my God. We gotta see if he's okay."

"No fucking way. Let's go."

"We can't just leave him."

"Somebody's probably called the cops already."

"Fuck fuck fuck fuck fuck. What if he's hurt really bad?"

"You just said you wanted to kill him."

"Not for real."

"Try telling that to a judge."

A porch light came on, then another. They could hear a siren.

As they watched, a man came out of the nearest house, loped to the truck, and helped Jefferson get out. Putting an arm around his waist, he guided him to the porch.

"He's okay. Now let's go."

They ran in a low crouch along the side of her house and into the half-wild backyard and started up the rock slope. Griff fumbled for a grip, pulled himself up, reached again for something to grab.

"It's better over here," Sonny said.

Griff dropped back down, then scrambled over to where Sonny had begun his climb. Using the crease in the rock face, he pulled himself up, secured another handhold, braced, and went higher. He was halfway there now.

"C'mon." Sonny was already at the top.

Griff pushed his right hand back into the crease and tensed his arm to take his weight. A sharp pain. Something—broken glass, it had to be—had sliced his fingertips.

"Fuck." Instinct yanked back his hand. His blood-slick fingers tried to find a new handhold, something to reestablish his balance. But his weight had shifted with his sudden movement, and a foot slipped. He was sliding now.

He scrabbled desperately over the rock face in search of something to grab. His left hand found a patch of moss, but when he gripped it, the vegetation came free.

His left foot hit hard on the base of the slope. Pain stabbed up his leg.

"Fuck, fuck, fuck."

A dog was barking now. Sonny came scrambling back.

"You okay?"

"Aggh. No. My ankle. Jesus Christ."

A back door opened. Lights came on.

"What the hell's going on out here?"

Another porch light came on, another door opened.

"Did you hear something, Ben?"

"No, but my dog's all worked up."

Sonny tugged at his arm.

"We gotta move, Griff."

"I don't think I can walk on it."

"You gotta. Give me the camera."

He pulled the straps over his head and pushed it Sonny's way.

The beam of a flashlight began to play across the ledges above them.

"I'll go that way." Sonny gestured to his left, in the direction they had come. "That'll distract 'em. You go along the bottom of the hill. Find a place to hide, then call me."

"I can't, dude. We'll just say we were looking for an owl, like you said."

But Sonny was already in motion. The dog's bark ripped the night air again, and the beam of light swung after him.

"Stop right there. I've got a gun."

Griff could feel nausea welling up inside him.

"Stop or I'll shoot."

"Oh sure you will," Sonny's mocking voice called back.

"Go get him, Cappy."

The dog was off its rope now, and Griff could hear it barking as it loped around, looking for a way up the slope. He had to go now, while the men were moving in the other direction.

He scrambled thirty feet on hands and knees until he came to a copse of trees. Grabbing one, he pulled himself up and hobbled forward. The second he put weight on his left foot, his ankle exploded in pain, forcing him down on his opposite knee.

He tried to make his steps smaller, quicker, but that didn't lessen the pain. Finally, he resorted to hopping on his good foot, leaning low and keeping his arms outstretched to catch himself if he fell. Moving that way, he made his way to the side of an outbuilding and rested there for a moment. His fingers were still bleeding, steadily if not profusely. He had wadded a piece of old T-shirt in his pants pocket to clean the camera lens, and he twisted that around his hand.

Only an upstairs light was on in the house ahead. A rake leaned against the porch railing. Dropping to his hands and knees, he crawled over and grabbed it.

Now he had something to take the weight his bad ankle wouldn't, and pushing hard on the handle, he limped across the street and through a vacant lot.

Two blocks distant from the ruckus, he paused again to catch his breath.

Three more blocks, and he was on Water Street. He waited behind some lilac bushes until a car passed, then lurched across the road and into the driveway of the Cannery, the pricey wharf-set summer restaurant, now closed for the season. He walked fifteen feet down its driveway and, hidden from the road by a tree, took out his cell and hit S for Sonny.

"Where are you?"

"Down by the Cannery. You?"

"Walking toward my house, just like any law-abiding citizen. The old man and Slut Butt are up in Calais tonight, so as soon as I get there, I'll take whatever car they left and come get you. I'll flash my lights so you'll know it's me."

Ten minutes later, a battered Ford Ranger came slowly over the rise. Seeing its lights blink, Griff limped from the bushes and pulled himself in.

"How you doing?"

"My ankle's fucked, and so are my fingers. Jesus, that was close."

"Nothing so exciting as a chase, is there?"

"That's excitement I can live without."

"You sound like a guy who needs a beer." Sonny reached back and passed him an already-opened bottle.

"You fucking idiot. If they stop us, you are royally fucked."

His friend laughed with studied nonchalance.

"Here's to living dangerously." He raised the bottle resting in his crotch. "Ahh. Just what the doctor ordered."

"You really are insane."

"Dude, we're good. Get your panties adjusted, have a swallow, and calm down."

Griff let the malty beer fill his mouth. Fear was giving way to annoyance, and annoyance to anger.

"Here's the thing. You weren't the one lying there hardly able to move."

Sonny shot him a sideways look.

"No. I'm the one who led 'em on a chase so you'd have time to get away. And then got the truck and came for you. So lighten up."

A thought hit him.

"Where's the camera?"

"I ditched it, just in case. But I hid it pretty good, in the woods. I'll get it tomorrow."

"Now I've gotta figure out how to explain my hand. And my ankle."

"One step ahead of you, Griff. Let's say you do it jogging home tonight."

"My folks will never believe that."

"They will if their dear boy calls from the scene of the accident, and they have to come get him."

Despite himself, Griff looked over admiringly.

"You're an evil genius."

Sonny brought his palms together like a movie star acknowledging applause.

"As for this other stuff, we gotta keep our mouths shut. No one can know."

"Really? I was thinking of calling the *Quoddy Tides*."

"I'm serious. Not a word to anybody, ever. Somebody's gonna notice Jefferson's tire was slashed, and then they'll know what caused the crash. Then the question is, who? We can't do anything that helps 'em connect the dots."

"Like I would."

"It happens when you aren't careful. In a few days, Sloggy will come back to school all bandaged up and wearing a neck brace, and everybody'll be wondering what the hell happened to him. Let's say you let it slip that he hit a hydrant, and that gets around. Pretty soon everybody'll get curious about how you knew."

"There's no fucking way I'd—"

"But more likely, a couple of years from now, you'll be wasted at a party, and somebody will mention Jefferson and what an asshole he was, and you'll want to tell them what we saw him do, and how you got him back. You'll think, nobody gives a rat's ass anymore, so you'll let it out. Oh, first you'll get a promise that they won't say anything, but sooner or later they will, and then that person will tell somebody else, and pretty soon, half the town will know. And then somebody'll get crosswise with the cops and need something to trade, and your little story will get told to Chief Tolland. Or maybe some do-gooder hears it, and their tender conscience makes 'em write an anonymous letter. Either way, what seemed like ancient history will become a real problem. So keep your mouth shut, okay?"

"Okay."

Sonny looked his way again, then took another sip of beer. When he spoke again, his normal jocularity had returned.

"I'll say this. When you get pissed, you're no longer mild-mannered Griff Kimball. You morph into the Dark Avenger, using the cloak of night to make the whole world right."

"Fuck you."

Yet deep down, those words brought a flush of pride.

Back at Sonny's, he sloshed some mouthwash around in his mouth, then Sonny dropped him off along the side of the Unitarian church property. Bracing for the coming pain, he scraped his fingers on the pavement to reopen the cut and then let himself tumble off the sidewalk where it fell a foot or so to the runnel at the edge of the churchyard. He lay there a minute, swearing mildly and moaning loudly, and then called home and told his mother that he'd tripped and sprained his ankle and couldn't walk.

She and his father arrived a few minutes later, alarm etched in their faces. His father helped him into the car while his mother rooted around in her purse for a package of Kleenex and gave him a wad to press his fingers against.

There was talk of taking him to the Calais hospital, but he insisted he'd be all right with ice and Advil and a bandage, and so he'd gone to bed amid the warm glow of parental attention.

The sprain was severe, but in some ways, that was a godsend. It meant basketball was out of the question for his junior year—and if you lost that season, nobody could expect you to play your senior year. Just too much ground to make up.

"Well, I've still got baseball," he'd said, trying to seem disappointed when the doctor delivered the news. "I'll just have to focus on that."

CHAPTER 31

WHEN SONNY STOPPED by the next afternoon, ostensibly to see how Griff was doing, he had bad news. The camera was gone.

"I know exactly where I put it," he said. "I hid it pretty well—at least I thought so last night. Somebody must've walked by and spotted it. What'd it cost?"

"New, five hundred dollars or so."

Sonny looked chagrined.

"Shit. I could give you half. I've got some cash that I've been saving to have my tooth fixed."

"Won't your dad pay for that?"

His friend shook his head.

"You'd think, but no. He says my mom should. She says she doesn't have the money. But it's been this way ever since eighth grade, so I guess I can put up with it for another year or two so's you can get a new camera."

Griff brushed the idea away with a hand gesture.

"Fuck it. I wasn't using it much anymore. Which reminds me of something." He reached into his desk drawer and took out the digital recorder. "Take this. I don't need it."

"Never used it?"

"Nope."

"But you're tempted by the shiny apple?"

"I don't want my mom finding it. She'd start pestering me about why I've got it. I might have to start working on the school newspaper."

"You can't fool me, Dark Avenger."

"Fuck you."

CHAPTER 32

JEFFERSON CAME BACK to school a week later wearing a neck brace, a cast on his left arm, and a large bandage on his forehead. Griff was outside when he walked stiffly by after the final bell and made his way to the parking lot. As he watched, Jefferson slowly folded himself into the passenger seat of Miss Laurent's idling Subaru.

"So I guess congratulations are in order, Dark Avenger," Sonny said when he told him. "You reunited your dream princess with her frog."

"We should let her know somebody knows what he did. Maybe then she'd leave him."

"Remember what I said. Not a fucking word. It'll only lead to trouble."

"I'm just talking an anonymous note. Something like, 'I was passing by one night and saw him hit you. I care about you. Please get help.'"

"Passing by? In her backyard?"

"She doesn't have to know that."

"She can figure out the sightlines, for fuck's sake. Where else could you have seen it from?"

"The thing is, maybe she'd report him if she knew other people knew."

"Or maybe she'd report that somebody's been looking in her window. And that they're probably the ones who slashed his tire."

"Somebody needs to do something. He's abusing her."

"That's what I like about you, Dark Avenger. Beneath your mild-mannered exterior, a flame of righteousness burns."

"I can't figure out why she's still with him."

Sonny knelt and pulled the beer bucket out from under the bed.

"There're a couple of possibilities. Maybe she had it coming, and she knows it."

"Next."

"Or maybe when she saw him all bleeding and dripping wet, she realized she loved old Sloggy in spite of it all."

"Don't call him that."

"Why not?"

"Because it makes him seem like he's just pathetic, when he's actually a fucking asshole."

Sonny took an elaborate drag on his cigarette, tilted his head theatrically, and blew the smoke out in a long thin line.

"Whatever. But there's a lesson there."

"What's that?"

"Things are what they are, and if you try to change 'em, you're just as likely to make 'em worse as better."

CHAPTER 33

STRANGELY, HIS INJURY had led to some limited athletic recognition, for if he wasn't much at basketball, he'd become a better-than-average baseball player. The gangliness that made him uncertain and awkward amid the quick organic flow of the basketball court was actually an advantage in the more deliberate process of pitching. He could throw the ball hard and accurately, and, free of Bobby's shadow, he'd put some real effort into improving. The squad wasn't outstanding, but it was plucky and competitive, and it wasn't the worst thing to be one of the stalwarts on a crew recognized for its scrappiness.

In the face of new camaraderie forged in joint competitive effort, his friendship with Sonny had faded some, for Sonny held baseball in the same lazy contempt as basketball.

"I've got to play to keep my folks happy," Griff said one day in study hall after his friend made a disdainful comment.

"Well, run along then and be a good boy," Sonny replied.

And yet, every so often he would call to check in, and then to add, "Just wondering if you want to drink some beer and take in the marvelous mysteries of Megan."

Drinking was breaking a pact the baseball team had made with one another. Yet most times, he'd gone.

And then Dan Winters, the crazy church lady's son, had come into his own. He'd ridden the bench for most of his freshman year, but you could tell his innate skills were starting to click. He had fought his way into the pitching rotation midway through his sophomore year, in part because he had a curve that worked, a rare thing for high-school baseball, and by season's end, he was getting the nod in more and more key games.

Watching him refine his control game by game, Griff sensed what would be next. Winters, a year behind him, would be the primary pitcher next season, and he, in his senior year, would be relegated to less important games and relief. Or maybe even asked to play center field.

Others didn't see it that way.

"He's good, Griff, but so are you," said Frank Cummings, the catcher. "When he's on, he's hard to hit, but he's still not as consistent as you are. Or as tricky. Besides, there's room for two star pitchers."

Except he knew he wasn't a star—and that Winters could be one. He was growing and throwing faster all the time. And he saw something in Winters he didn't feel in himself: an all-consuming desire to play, to win, to prevail.

"They say he goes out and pitches every night into an old tire," he told Sonny one day when he'd drunk enough to confide his fear of being upstaged. "I mean, I like baseball, but not *that* much."

"Once you get out of high school, none of it amounts to a pile of crap," Sonny said, his half-lidded look signaling his utter boredom with the topic.

Sonny was right, really. Who knew or cared a few years on? Except the former players themselves who, like in the Bruce Springsteen song, endlessly relived their glory days when three or four of them found themselves together.

So, he'd taken comfort in his pal's view. And later, when he'd decided not to play his senior year, only to discover indifference and distance replacing the camaraderie he'd had with his teammates, he'd quickly settled back into the easy groove of their friendship.

CHAPTER 34

SUSAN EXTENDED HER arms like wings, then brought her hands back in front of her with twin zeros fashioned by thumbs and forefingers.

"This is how much I care about what Griff Kimball thinks of me. Anybody who hangs out with Sonny Beal has got to be a mega-loser. He's like Gollum in the Hobbit movies, always slithering around trying to look down your blouse." She scrunched up her face and wiggled her tongue. "We likes what we sees my precious, oh yes, we does. But we wants to see more, my precious, and we knows we never will. Not without our ring, which makes us invisible."

Jenna giggled, then resumed the indignant attitude of someone outraged on her friend's behalf.

"Even if he was invisible, I'd know he was looking at me. He's a maximum creeper."

"And the way he smokes." Susan brought two fingers to her lips, tilted her head back, then pursed her lips and feigned an extended exhalation of smoke. "Who does that? Besides the Nazis, I mean."

Jenna broke into such a hearty laugh that she fell back on the bed.

"I could tell Griff off for you."

"It's not worth wasting the words. Griff doesn't know the first thing about me. Besides, he's a total hypocrite. He sits behind me in consumer science, and he's all friendly and everything. What's that about if he thinks I'm a slut?"

"Maybe he wants to hook up and meant it as a compliment."

They lapsed into frenetic laughter.

"Did your brother say who told the McKinney guy that Griff said that about me?"

"I guess Griff told the judge that's what he said that made Dan go crazy on him."

Susan frowned.

"That's weird, too. I mean, why does Dan care? It's not like we're even friends anymore."

And yet, after they'd broken up he had still said hi when they passed in the hall, and she did still turn occasionally to find him looking at her. He was going away in a day or two, because of the fight, going to Portland or Augusta or wherever the State sent problem kids.

And all because of her.

She decided she should go see him before he left.

CHAPTER 35

SHE HAD SWITCHED seats in consumer science so that she was no longer near Griff, but she hadn't confronted him regarding his comment about her.

When someone mentioned it to her, she'd make a funny face.

"I mean, like he'd know whether I'm a slut. Or whether anyone else is, for that matter."

Then one morning, making her way from CS to trig, she noticed him standing at the top of the stairs. She crossed to the other side and made her way up through the kids coming down, but when she reached the last step, he was waiting for her.

"Can I talk to you?"

"No."

"Just for a second?"

She stared icily at him.

"What part of *no* don't you get?"

"Two minutes. Then I'll never bother you again."

She shifted her books to the opposite arm and leaned lightly against the wall.

"I know it's going around that I was bad-mouthing you, but I wasn't."

"Everybody thinks so."

"I know. But it's not true."

Mr. Morton, the chemistry teacher, walked by, trailing the smell of a just-smoked cigarette.

"Second bell's about to ring. You two better get to class."

"Another demerit and I've got detention. But I just wanted to tell you that."

"Why should I believe it?"

"I could tell you, later."

"I thought two minutes was all you needed."

He raised his hands in a palms-up appeal.

"Maybe tonight, on the breakwater?"

She was about to say no when the long strident buzz of the second bell sounded.

"Please? I'll be there at eight."

He set off running down the hall.

She slipped into class just as Mr. Tedecci walked over to shut the door.

CHAPTER 36

SHE HADN'T PLANNED to go, yet the more she thought about it, the more it seemed silly not to hear him out. Maybe he hadn't said it. After all, why would he think that? It wasn't like she hooked up or sexted naked photos of herself. And while half the girls in the junior class were having sex of one kind or another, the most she'd ever done was parade around for Dan Winters. She had nothing to be ashamed of.

She waited until 8:25, then walked out on the pier, doubting he'd have hung out for that long. If not, then whatever he wanted to say must not be that important.

There was his pickup, about midway down.

"Can we take a ride?"

She hesitated a moment but then opened the passenger door and got in. Sitting there with him would set small-town tongues wagging, and that prospect made her self-conscious.

"Gleason's Cove?" he said.

It was a picnic spot maybe eight miles away, by the shore in Perry and relatively private.

"I've got to be home by ten."

"No problem."

His truck smelled like weed.

"Are you stoned?"

"It's not mine. Sonny did a joint after school."

"Just him?"

"Just him. Really."

She let that go without a reply. When they got to Gleason's, he found an out-of-the-way spot and stopped the truck. The setting sun had left the western sky a muted violet streaked with magenta where cirrus clouds caught a different shade of light, a stark contrast to the dark water in front of them.

"Wow, that's worth the drive," she said, to break the ice.

"Sometimes the skies here are amazing. And we just take it all for granted."

The remark surprised her.

"Do you still take pictures?"

"Not so much anymore, now that everyone does." He held up his phone, made a face, and pretended to take a selfie.

"So that's that? I mean, with the skies everyone else takes for granted?"

He eyed her uncertainly.

"My camera got wet. I need to get it to Bangor to have it fixed." He glanced at the sky. "You want a beer while we watch it fade? I've got some in the back."

How did guys find it so easy to get beer? She was lucky if she could sneak an occasional one from the fridge.

"They're Sonny's too, I suppose."

"Zing. No, all mine."

"I'd rather have an explanation."

"It's a two-for-one deal."

"Since you put it that way."

He got out and fished around in the back and brought back a couple of sweating Budweiser twelve-ouncers. Popping his, he took a long gulp. She cleaned the groove with her fingernail and wiped the top on her sleeve, then opened it and took a sip.

"So anyway, thanks for coming," he said after a minute. "Like I said, I know what's going around, but I never called you a slut."

"Didn't you tell the judge you did?"

"I said it was something like that. But it wasn't."

"What did you say then?"

"Just a guy thing."

"But what?"

"It was just kind of a . . . a baseball joke, about you getting his fastball, high and inside."

"Getting his fast . . . That is *so* dumb."

"I know. I'm sorry."

"Why would you even say that? We weren't. Not that it's any of your business."

"I don't know. It just kind of came out. I really am sorry."

She took another drink of beer.

"You're telling the truth?"

"I swear. Sonny was there. Ask him."

"Like I'd believe that weirdo."

"He's all right."

"Everyone I know thinks he's a creep. Nobody can figure out why you hang out with him."

"Maybe I see something everybody else misses."

"Or maybe you miss something everybody else sees."

Griff laughed, seemingly at ease for the first time since she had gotten into his truck.

"Well, maybe. But you believe me?"

"I don't know."

"It's true. Really. God strike me dead."

She took another sip of beer and then glanced ostentatiously around the sky, as though waiting for a lightning bolt.

"So are we okay? I'd like to be friends again. I mean, I know it's not like we were tight or anything, but I'd like to be that way again." He blushed. "God, I sound like an idiot."

"Maybe you're drunk."

"This is my first one."

"Maybe you're a lightweight."

His puzzled look made her smile.

"Kidding, Griff, kidding."

A rueful smile came to his face.

"But we're okay?"

She ran her hand through her hair, tucking a strand back behind her ears.

"If you didn't say it, why did you tell the judge you did?"

"I was nervous, and I was just kind of paraphrasing."

"And why did Dan got so upset?"

"You got me. Maybe because he's freaking looney tunes."

But he didn't meet her eyes when he spoke, and for the first time that night, she thought he was lying.

CHAPTER 37

HER SENSE THAT Griff was hiding something piqued her interest. Not in him, exactly, but in discovering what it was.

That was the reason she lowered her window when, a week or so later, he pulled his pickup alongside her car on the breakwater; the reason why, when he said he was going to Calais on Friday to see a movie—a film, he called it—with Keira Knightley in it, she had said yes to his invitation.

She hadn't been in an actual theater in months, and she thought she could coax it out of him during the thirty-mile drive to Calais. But the conversation had settled onto other things on the way up, and it was only natural to talk about the movie on the trip home. She had found it unsatisfying because of its harsh ending, but he'd liked it because he thought it was truthful. That, he said, was a refreshing change of pace for films that made it to Downeast Maine; they were usually sentimental, because that's all that could fill theaters outside of Portland.

"Why can't rural people be as sophisticated as city people?"

"Self-selection, maybe. Or maybe, because life is tough up here, we need to believe everything works out in the end. Or maybe we're afraid of the truth."

"That's a mighty big mess of maybes, mister."

He chuckled.

"I've got lots of theories, but I can't ever decide if any of them are right."

She tried to think of a movie she'd seen in Calais that disproved his point but couldn't.

"Are you going to leave when you graduate?"

"No."

"So what are you going to do?"

"Get a smart TV and a subscription to Hulu."

It wasn't until he offered a sly smile that she realized he was kidding.

"No, really."

"Work for my father, I guess." He grimaced. "I know I should have big plans to go to college, move away and all that, but I like it here. You probably think that's lame."

"No."

She found it reassuring, actually. Some of her friends were talking about leaving, about going to college and then to Portland or Boston or even New York City. She'd only been to Boston once and never to New York. The mere thought of all that traffic, all those people, intimidated her. She didn't want to live in a city.

"I like it here too," she said. "I just wish I'd lived someplace else for a while, so I'd have something to compare Eastport to. I mean, not like Calais or Machias or Bangor but some other state, just so I'd have a better idea. It'd be awful to go somewhere when you're sixty and wish you'd spent your whole life there."

By the time they had exhausted the topic, a trip that could sometimes seem endless was almost over, and bringing up Dan would have seemed calculated.

She worried he'd try to kiss her when he dropped her off.

"Well, good-bye, and thanks," she said, preemptively, as his truck rolled to a stop in front of her house.

"Sorry you didn't like the film."

"I didn't hate it. I just didn't like the ending."

"Fun to talk about, anyway."

"Yeah," she said. And she meant it.

When he called a week later to see if she wanted to do something, she said she had a cold, which she did, or at least the beginning of one, half hoping, half fearing that would end things.

The next time she heard from him, it was by text: "Question for you, want 2 see best pic w/me?"

"I don't text and date," she'd shot back—and was surprised when, a few seconds later, he called to invite her over to watch *One Flew Over the Cuckoo's Nest*, which he said was "far and away" his favorite film.

It was hard to see how she'd have the opportunity to find out what she wanted sitting there in his family's rec room, with his parents probably hovering nearby. But after what he'd said about sentimentality, she was interested in a movie—a film—he called his favorite.

Besides, no other guy had shown any interest in her since Dan had been sent away. Maybe, after the pounding he'd given Griff, fear had them keeping their distance.

Which made it all the odder that Griff himself didn't seem to worry—and left her feeling even more strongly that there was something she didn't know.

"That is a great movie," she said when the credits spooled across the screen.

"I'm glad you think so."

"But the chief—isn't it sentimental to have him redeemed that way?" she said later, as they walked to her house.

"I guess. I never said I was an absolutist."

They stood outside her door talking for a few minutes more. When he seemed ready to say another casual good night, she brought her face to his and kissed him.

CHAPTER 38

IT WASN'T UNTIL months later that she got the secret out of Griff, and by then, they were in a relationship.

At first, the sheer unlikeliness of it all had made their time together seem destined to end of its own accord. And yet it hadn't. Instead, they had started seeing each other regularly.

At night in her room, when she did a rough appraisal of where they stood on the desirability scale, she found her calculation undergoing a subtle shift. Yes, she was more popular than he was, but in the friends-with-everyone way of a girl who would don an orange vest and a black leotard and paint her face for the Shead Tigers alumni game, earning an appreciative laugh from the entire school, and that kind of popularity mattered less and less to her as she neared the end of her junior year.

She was, she knew, the archetypal girl next door: pretty in a perky, wholesome way, but hardly sultry and certainly not beautiful. The young woman who stared back from her full-length mirror was someone you'd describe as "in shape," something she worked at, rather than "shapely," which she longed to be. She was slim enough, but not bewitchingly slender in the way of some long-legged classmates. She wasn't flat-chested, but neither was she bosomy in that deep-cleavagey way that was a magnet for male eyes.

She'd be one of those women who aged slowly, whose former classmates would say, twenty years on, "You look exactly the same as you did in high school" and who would be fibbing only a little. Friends said that to her mother now, and she knew from photos it was close to the truth.

She should be grateful for those genes; she knew that, too. And yet there were times when she'd have signed a pact with the devil to be plump at fifty if only she could have Maria Marlson's curvy figure now. Or Alyson Dolph's marvelous cheekbones and long, perfect legs. Or Bonnie Rogers' bee-stung lips and blouse-filling boobs.

She was tired of being the girl guys confided their relationship woes to. She wanted them to fixate on her the way they did on Maria and Alyson and Bonnie. She had seen the desire in Dan's eyes as she'd twirled before him, and his look had triggered a heady rush of amorous delight—until things had gotten out of hand.

Now she was surprised at how appealing she found Griff's angular looks, his brown eyes, his sly wit. It was like opening an unassuming book in a secondhand store and idly scanning the first few paragraphs and then finding yourself so engrossed you couldn't stop reading.

After a month, she abandoned the idea that their relationship was "a lark with an arc," as she had joked when first revealing to a stunned Jenna that she and Griff were going out. After three, she decided she was ready to sleep with Griff and found herself disappointed when things didn't seem to be progressing that way. She'd taken to wearing spaghetti-strap tops to make things easy for him. That had worked, but he was passive about pushing further, as though he feared offending her. He seemed content to make out on the breakwater, where the periodic sweep of headlights from out-for-a-drive townsfolk, and even occasional walkers, prevented extended intimacy.

On one of the nights when she drove, she had taken him to the parking spot she and Dan had frequented. She had made a game of it, ordering him to close his eyes when they were still in the Middle End, as central Eastport was oddly called, and making him try to guess where they were going. She didn't allow him to open them until she had taken the seldom-used lane through the cemetery to the war memorial and parked up behind it.

"Wow, this is a whole other world. How'd you even know about it?"

Ready for that query, she had spun a tale about going to the flower shop to buy a birthday bouquet for her grandmother when a delegation of VFW members had been retrieving floral arrangements for Memorial Day and how one had asked her if she'd ever visited the town's tribute to its service members.

"I promised I would," she said. "I didn't tell him I didn't even know about it."

But the newfound privacy hadn't spurred him on to anything more.

It was baffling. Dan had wanted to go all the way with her, but when she had rebuffed him, he'd broken things off, saying she was too good for him. Now Griff seemed disinclined even to try for actual sex or anything close to it. It left her wondering whether there was something about her that made her seem too goody-goody for guys to think about that way.

Some nights, after another evening together that hadn't gotten them any closer to doing it, she lay in bed and thought of the high-school couples she knew who were having sex regularly, of the exasperation her girlfriends affected when discussing how much their boyfriends wanted it, of the delight they took in getting them all worked up early in the evening and then forcing them to endure a party or a movie or even a night of TV with younger siblings before finally allowing themselves to be spirited away for intimate interludes.

In those moments, she worried her own love life would never truly begin.

CHAPTER 39

SUSAN TILTED THE dark green bottle, and they watched as the sparkling wine frothed up to the edge of the Dixie cups.

"I was sure we had some plastic champagne flutes out here. Mom must have done something with them."

They were at her family's cottage on Pennamaquan Lake on a night when her parents were busy at a retirement party.

"Anyway, happy nineteenth, Griff. I am now officially dating an older man."

Susan raised her cup. He touched it with his and took a sip.

"I can't believe you got this. Where'd it come from?"

"It's got to be from the Champagne region of France to be called champagne."

"Zing." He pulled an imaginary dart from his arm. "Did you steal it from your folks?"

"Nope."

"From Jenna's?"

"They don't drink."

"C'mon, tell me."

"Then I'd have to kill you. And on your birthday. Think how that would look on your headstone."

"Well, it's great. All this is."

She spread her hands out over the cottage table and laughed.

"Pretty hard to mess up artichokes. Unless you forget the butter."

"Where'd you hide that?" His eyes were on the shimmery black dress she wore.

"In the picnic basket. Notice anything different?"

He cast an uncertain look over her face and then down to her neck and shoulders.

"New earrings?"

"Warm."

Griff eyed the amber pendant she wore in the V of the dress.

"The necklace."

"Cooler."

"Perfume?"

"Cold."

"I give up."

"Griff, I got my hair cut."

"Oh God, of course," he said, genuinely chagrined. "But you had your Red Sox hat on. Until just a minute ago."

"You like it?"

"Love it."

"Really?"

"Really."

"Good, 'cause I needed a change. I don't want to look like the girl next door anymore."

"Why not?"

She brought her lips to his ear.

"Because I want to be the hottie next door."

"Mission accomplished."

When they were done with the meal, she collected the plates and carried them into the camp's rustic kitchen.

"Time for your presents," she said, refilling their Dixie cups with champagne. "Can you put some more wood on the fire?"

When he bent to feed the fire they'd lit to take the edge off the cool in the September air, she downed her cup and refilled it.

"Here's the first one," she said, coming to where he sat.

He ripped the wrapping off and opened the thin cardboard box to reveal an L.L.Bean brushed-flannel shirt in black watch plaid.

"To keep you warm on your winter-morning oil deliveries."

He rubbed the material against his face.

"Wow. It's so soft. Thanks, Susan."

"This one's next."

Moving in front of the fire, she watched as he tore the birthday paper off. He stared for a second at the unmistakable logo on the blue box and then looked at her.

"And now for your big present."

Crossing her arms in front of her the way she had practiced so many times, she slipped the dress's thin straps from her shoulders. The black satin slid down her body and puddled around her ankles. She stood naked before him.

She came to him and put her arms around his neck, and they kissed. She could hear his breath growing ragged, could feel her own heart pounding. She unbuttoned his shirt, and when it was undone, he pulled it off, then kicked off his shoes and scrambled out of his jeans. He fumbled a minute with the condom, and then he was on top of her.

It didn't happen with the swept-away passion of the movies or the animal urgency of the pornos that she'd seen—that everyone had seen—on the Internet. It hurt at first, hurt so much that she gasped.

"You okay?"

"Mmm-hmmm."

The pain grew sharper, and she had to brace her arms against his stomach.

"Should I stop?"

"No. Just slow."

She took her hands away and felt the increasing weight of his body and the thrust of his hips. After a minute, he moaned and pushed faster and faster and then moaned again and apparently was done, and she lay there under him, both glad and sorry it was over.

"That was so good. Are you all right?"

"I think so. It hurts . . ."

"Bad?"

"Just a little. Let's have more champagne."

"I'll get it."

He scrambled up, hand half covering himself, and went to the kitchen.

She put his shirt on, fastening only two buttons, and slipped away to the bathroom.

Blood was trickling down her thigh. She wiped it off with some folded toilet paper and daubed gingerly at herself, then looked at her face in the mirror and smiled.

He was on the couch when she emerged, bare-chested but with his pants on.

He held out a cup of champagne.

"To us."

"To us."

She took a sip, then set her cup down atop a pile of old *Reader's Digest*s. She kissed him, lightly at first, and then more passionately.

"Are you sure you want to get dressed so soon?"

"Was it better that time?" he said when they were done and he lay behind her, her body pulled close to his, his arms wrapped around her.

"Mmm-hmmm."

"Really?"

"Really," she said, then laughed. "Really *really*."

"God, I'm lucky."

She reached back and squeezed his arms.

"You know what's weird?" he said.

"What?"

"If it wasn't for him—for Winters—we wouldn't be together."

She knew that was true, yet it was something she was reluctant to acknowledge.

"I don't know. We used to talk in math class."

"Yeah, but it wouldn't have gone anywhere. What would you have said if I'd asked you out? I mean, without me taking you out to Gleason's to explain how I'd never said you were a slut."

"I am now," she giggled. "So maybe you could just see into the future."

"But really, would you have gone out with me?"

"I mean, probably not. But I didn't know you."

"It's strange how things happen."

Susan rolled over so they were face-to-face.

"I still don't get why what you said bothered him so much."

When he didn't reply, she spoke again.

"There's something you didn't tell me, isn't there?"

He frowned.

"I just don't feel like . . . like it would be fair."

"You're worried about being fair to him?"

"You promise you won't tell anyone? Even if we break up, which I hope never happens?"

"Uh-huh."

He bit his lower lip, took a deep breath, exhaled, then looked her in the eye.

"His father was a rapist. That's how his mother got pregnant."

"What? How do you know that?"

"Sonny heard it in Lubec. His mother, the church lady, grew up there. She moved here after a sailor raped her."

"Oh my God."

"What?"

"That explains . . . some things."

"He didn't . . ."

She shook her head.

"No. But he . . . he tried. I mean, kind of."

Later, she wondered whether she had exaggerated. She had left out her dance, substituting "messing around a little" for the moments before Dan had entered her room.

But she had had to bite his lip and yell to get him to stop. There was no doubt about that.

She thought of the way he had grabbed her, pulled her to him, forced his mouth on hers.

Maybe she had been closer to something terrible than she had realized at the time.

CHAPTER 40

IT WAS ONLY a few days later that Dan's letter arrived.

>Hi Susan,
>
>I know it was quite a while ago that you asked me to write, but I've been thinking a lot about you lately, so anyways, here goes.
>
>I hope you are well and that everything is good at school and with your family. I'd say to say hi for me, but I guess that would be awkward. I wish I could say things are okay here, but I hate this place. Some of these guys are real badasses. They are in gangs, and they say part of the initiation is just walking up to someone on the street and sucker-punching them.
>
>One guy claims he and his friends stole, like, thirty cars before they got caught. Jaguars and Beamers and Audis and ones like that. He says they got paid to do it because they're too young to go to jail (real jail, anyway) and that they made $1,000 for each car.
>
>Another one says he and his gang beat the hell out of somebody who ratted on them for breaking into a store. He says they clubbed him with a tire iron until he passed out. Another guy claims he knifed someone.
>
>They might just be talking, I don't know. But one night, some of them held a blanket over a kid nobody likes, and another guy punched him until he was just sobbing and begging them to stop. Nobody will say who did it, because then it will happen to you. You've always got to be on your guard for stuff like that.
>
>Some of them asked me why I'm in here, and I told

them I lost it and beat up somebody so bad that he was in the hospital for, like, a month, which is kind of an exaggeration, but I'm hoping it will keep them from messing with me. I had one dream that I had actually killed him and had to stay here for the rest of my life. Then when I woke up, things didn't seem so bad!

I have to go once a week and talk to a therapist about controlling my anger and how I feel about what I did. I know everybody in Eastport thinks I'm an ax murderer or something, but I don't think what I did is even close to the stuff these guys have done. Or say they did. That wasn't what he wanted to hear. He says I'm not taking responsibility. But it's how I feel. Kimball was ragging me, and I lost it and let him have it. But he started it. I never did anything to get him on my case. The guy is just a complete a-hole. And I'm the one paying the price. I didn't even get a lawyer or anything because my mother thought the Lord would take care of it. (I guess he was doing something else that day.)

The good news (if you can call it that) is that I'm in school here, and the classes are okay. It's different from Shead. No one says anything in class because they're worried they'll piss people off and get a blanket beat-down. Still, I'll be able to get a high-school diploma, so maybe I can join the service or something.

Anyways (I guess I already said that), I'd like to hear from you if you want to write. I know things didn't turn out that well with us, but I think about you a lot. I try to follow the Shead teams, but it's hard to get any news, so if you have anything from the *Quoddy Tides* you could send, I'd appreciate it.

Thanks for reading this.

Dan

Susan read the letter again.

She had completely forgotten asking Dan to write, and now she was angry that he had. After all, she had said that back when she thought he'd done what he'd done out of some crazy sense that he had to defend her honor. And he'd let her think that, even though it hadn't been that way at all. Maybe he'd just assumed she'd never find out. But she had, and as far as she was concerned, that had changed everything.

She couldn't write and say she was going out with Griff. She just couldn't. Yet she couldn't write him without saying that, either.

She thought about composing a short note saying she had changed her mind, that she no longer wanted to hear from him. But how would she explain that?

The best thing was just not to answer. Maybe then he'd figure out that she'd learned the truth.

Even if he didn't, Dan was too proud to persist in the face of silence. Unless reform school had changed him. Certainly the Dan she'd known would have been.

So in the end, she tucked the letter under a stack of T-shirts in her dresser and did nothing.

CHAPTER 41

TAKING A DEEP breath, Dan walked the final few steps and looked into the casket. For a few seconds, on a subconscious level, he wondered whether a mistake had been made, so different did the face there seem from the one in his memory. Only slowly did he start to distinguish her lineaments tracing like palimpsest through the heavy makeup. It was like a chance meeting with an acquaintance from years ago, someone you vaguely recognize but whose features no longer bring back a name or place of association.

Was it because she had been transfigured by death into a repose she had never possessed in life? Or because he hadn't seen her in the last year and a half?

They had dressed her in an outfit nicer and newer than anything he could remember her wearing. Was it hers or a final act of charity from the church? The ruffled blouse fit snugly over the contours of her body, and he found himself surprised that his mother had had such big breasts. Perhaps the baggy tops she had favored had been chosen to disguise that. Had she, after her hookup with Fortin, ever known a male touch? Nothing he'd ever heard from her or anyone else even hinted at it. Her story, then, had in all likelihood robbed her life of any intimacy.

Those thoughts had crept in unbidden, and when he realized what he was contemplating, he gave his head a quick, hard shake. And yet, hadn't that long-ago lie determined everything? It had prompted her move to Eastport and, eventually, into the insistent embrace of the church. It had influenced his entire life, dictating the meagerness of their existence and instilling in him the envy and shame and want, if not the actual hard hunger, of real poverty.

He had lived with the humiliating sense of being poor as long as he could remember. He thought now of the day he had come home from the third grade, choking back sobs after Albee Dotton had let slip why he hadn't been able to invite him to his sleepover.

"His mother is worried I might have lice, 'cause my hair is all uneven and greasy, and lots of poor people get it."

"Don't you listen to him, Danny. That may not be my best haircut, but your hair isn't greasy, and you don't have lice. And we're not poor." She drew his tear-swollen face to her, but though he'd wanted the comfort of her hug, a part of him rebelled.

"Then why do we live here? And why don't you do things like other kids' moms, instead of working for the stupid church?"

"Well, I'm me, and I'm a different story," his mother replied. "But you're just as good as any of them, Danny, and you remember that. A boy with your talents can be anything you want to be. It's all up to you."

The next day, she had taken him to the barber.

"I tried to do it myself, and I guess I didn't do much of a job," she said as Mr. Harper surveyed his uneven locks. "Can you make it look nice?"

That night after supper, she had stacked the dishes on the counter.

"These can wait," she said. "I thought maybe you'd like the hot water for a bath." He knew from experience that the dull copper tank, which relied on an element in the stove for heat, couldn't fill the tub with more than five or six inches of hot water.

"There's never enough."

"Well, then, we'll just heat some extra," she said. She'd dug the spaghetti pot from under the sink, filled it and the teakettle, and set them to heating on the stove.

"I'll need more than that."

"Then you'll get it. I'll just keep bringing it in until you say enough." And she had. He had spent an indolent evening soaking up to his ears in a luxury of hot water, lingering so long that, having heard the back door squeak on its hinges, he had peered through the crescent his hand cut across the fogged window to see her squatting to pee in the dark backyard.

"I'm going for a walk."

Mr. Grantley, the funeral director, nodded.

"You've got a good half an hour before the guests start to show up. It'll be easier then, don'tcha know?"

He wondered if anyone would really come to visiting hours for an eccentric woman who had lived an otherworldly existence in a tiny house there in the North End. But by the time he returned three-quarters of an hour later, five or six people were talking outside the funeral parlor.

A jowly man in a well-tailored suit stepped forward and extended his hand.

"Hello, Daniel. I'm Abner Peevers. I'm very sorry for your loss. For our loss."

"Thank you."

"Your mother was quite a woman, always so generous."

"She didn't have much to be generous with."

"She had her time, and perhaps that's the greatest gift of all. So many people relied on her. Shut-ins in want of company, the infirm who were hungry for a homemade meal, elderly ladies in need of a ride to the grocery store. I must say, she brought a lot of people to the faith that way, yes, she did. She was one of the Lord's true shepherds. She'll be missed."

His mother, an offbeat religion's outreach recruiter. Give me your poor, your downtrodden, your huddled masses yearning for a lift to the IGA . . .

Peevers reached into the pocket of his suit jacket and pulled out a set of keys.

"Her car is up at Finney's Exxon. He'd been working on it, but it's fixed now. The church took care of the bill."

"Thanks."

"Have you decided whether you want me to be your voice at the service, Dan?"

"Why don't you just say what you want? I think the church was her real family."

Moving inside before the man could say more, he was surprised to find the room half-full. He circulated around, introducing himself to some of the assembled and participating in the give-and-take of grieving.

"Your mother was the finest kind," said one elderly woman who kept his hand pressed between her brittle fingers as she spoke. "In the last two years of my sister's life, your mother did more for her than her own children. Maude told me she loved her like her own flesh and blood."

She leaned forward conspiratorially.

"She had a little money set away, and she wanted to leave your mother the same share her daughters were getting. You know why she didn't?"

"No, ma'am."

"Your mother wouldn't hear of it. She said, 'I'm here because I'm your friend. What you have should go to your family.' Not many would do that. She didn't have much herself."

"I know."

"Well, yes, of course you do, dear. I'm so sorry for your loss."

He moved to the back of the room and took a seat there.

An elderly man approached and, arm shaking with Parkinson's, gripped his hand fiercely.

"Your mother drove me to Calais three times a week when my wife fell and had to go to the rehabilitation place," he said. "With all the bills, I could hardly pay for gas, let alone give her anything for her time."

A commotion came from near the door. The group parted to admit a woman in an electric wheelchair. Her head was canted to the right, and her lips jerked spasmodically. She used the hand controls to back her chair in a wide arc and then bring it alongside the coffin. Holding herself up on her elbows, she heaved her body forward to peer down into the coffin. After half a minute, she lapsed back into the chair and struggled to make the sign of the cross. Her lips opened and closed rapidly now, and her chest heaved in echoing spasms. She was weeping, he realized—weeping for his mother.

Someone tapped his elbow, and he turned quickly that way.

"Hi, Dan."

"Hi. Thanks for coming. She would have appreciated it."

The woman, slim, brown-haired, with hazel eyes—now where had he seen her before?—looked quizzically at him.

"I didn't really know your mother, I'm sorry to say."

"Oh. Well . . ." His face must have betrayed his confusion.

"Dan, I'm Shirley Jameison, Susan's mother. I'm here because Agnes Holmes needed a ride." She gestured toward the woman in the electric wheelchair. "Your mother was awfully good to her, and she was determined to come."

"Oh, Mrs. Jameison. Sorry I didn't recognize you. It's been . . ." He let the words trail off.

"How are you doing?"

"I'm okay."

"I hear you're at Bates now."

"Yeah."

"That's terrific. Really. You like it?"

He nodded. "Yeah. It's hard—a lot harder than Shead—but I'm learning loads. How's Susan?"

"She's . . . she's good."

"Is she off at college?"

"No, still at home. But she's going to WCCC."

"I thought she was thinking of UMaine."

"She was, but she's pretty serious with Griff and all . . ."

"With Griff? Griff Kimball?"

Mrs. Jameison bit her lip.

"They've been together for a while. I thought you knew."

"How long?"

"A year or so at least."

He shook his head.

"Susan and Griff. Wow. Who'd have believed it?"

"I know you and Griff had your problems, but I have to say, he treats her very well and . . ."

His eyes narrowed.

"We didn't 'have our problems.' Our only problem was him shooting his mouth off for no reason. I never did a single thing to provoke him."

Mrs. Jameison looked at her feet.

"I'm sorry, I shouldn't have brought any of this up—not at a time like this. I just assumed you knew."

"I wish I had."

He felt a tug on his sleeve and turned to find an older woman with immaculately done hair leaning on a tripod cane.

"Are you Clara's son?"

"Yes."

"I'm Marion Taylor. Your mother used to make me supper sometimes."

Mrs. Jameison squeezed his other arm. "Good-bye, Dan," she said and slipped away.

"As part of the church program?" he asked.

"No, I didn't belong to her church. She did it out of the goodness of her heart, came over to cook and tell me the news around town."

"Did she try to get you to join?"

She shook her head.

"My people were Congregationalists, and her bunch was always too shouty for me. She knew that. We used to laugh about it." She looked at him with antique eyes. "You aren't one, are you?"

"No."

"I didn't think so, not a boy who went off to one of those fancy colleges. Anyway, I want you to know how sorry I am. She had a heart of gold." She patted his arm. "If it helps any, she was always talking about you—how well you were doing and how she wished she could have done more for you growing up. The sun rose and set on you as far as your mom was concerned."

"Thank you, ma'am."

He heard a whir and looked up to see the woman in the wheel-chair steering it his way. She stopped next to him.

"Daaaa-nnny?" she said, her tremulous falsetto pushing weirdly at his name.

"Yes."

"I loooo-vvved yer maaa-ahrrmm."

"Thank you."

She reached a shaking hand to his sleeve and laid it on his wrist.

"She was prahhh-per proud of yo-oou, Daaaa-nnny. Prahh-per proud."

He nodded.

"May you be as goooo-oood as shhh-hee was, Daaaa-nnny."

"Thank you."

With that, she was gone, rolling down the aisle toward the coffin for a final look.

Feeling a need for the cold bite of outside air, he made his way as quickly as he could through the gathering and out into the darkening afternoon. It was a relief to challenge his legs on the steep hill that led to the high school.

A group of teens stood talking near the front entrance. He angled away from them, crossed the road, and walked to the elementary school and then behind it to the baseball diamond.

The ground was spongy but thawed, the smell of the wet sod familiar and comforting. The light was fading quickly now, the outline of home plate becoming hard to see from his perch on the pitcher's mound.

"Bet I could still catch the corner with a curve," he said aloud.

And he could. It was something he had, not quite magical but special.

He knew he had to go back, yet he let himself drift off the wet turf and climb the rocky escarpment that overlooked the field. From that promontory, he could see the silhouette of the Lubec bridge, its lights a distant beacon marking the narrow span of his mother's life.

A place so near when traveling by water but so far by land that she could take refuge within its very sight.

He stood on the damp rock and watched as the fog drifted in. Somewhere out in the bay, a bell buoy clanged. Had she ever stood here and gazed at her past? Had she ever felt his desperate longing to find someplace where you could lose your past without sacrificing your future—or had that all seemed too much for her to hope for?

By the time he had returned, the group in the funeral home had thinned to about a dozen. He slipped in the back, slid onto one of the folding chairs, and bowed his head as if in prayer, hoping no one would disturb him.

When he looked up some minutes later, the room was empty except for one woman who sat in the first row of chairs. He couldn't recall ever seeing her before. Her brown hair was close-cropped, her smallish mouth just now pursed in thought or sorrow.

Perhaps sensing his gaze, she turned and met his eye. She rose and walked toward him.

"Are you Dan?"

"Yeah."

"I didn't want to disturb you while you were praying. I'm Fern Blanchard. I was a friend of your mother's. I want you to know how sorry I am."

"Thank you."

"Sometimes life can be awfully hard."

"It sure can. Did you know her from the church?"

"No, from Lubec. We went to high school together."

She sat down beside him.

"I say I was a friend, but I guess I really wasn't much of one. Once she moved here, she never came back to Lubec, so far as I know. And I only ever made it over once or twice to visit. But when I heard, I had to come and say good-bye."

"Well, thanks for coming. I was thinking tonight what a long way it is for a place that's so close."

"I know. The Maine coast. Nothing like it."

She fell silent for a minute, then started speaking in a rush.

"That's not why I didn't visit more often. Your mother changed after it happened."

She stopped abruptly.

"Oh God . . . I haven't . . . You do know what happened?"

"Yes."

"Thank goodness." She threw her head back in relief. "It would have been so awful to have . . . and at her funeral." She paused for a moment, then continued.

"Anyway, after that, she was just different. The town wasn't very kind. The guy who did it had some friends, some shipmates, from Lubec, and they all said she'd made it up. And the old biddies acted like it was her fault even if she was raped, and some of the not-so-old biddies, too. Honestly, I think even her grandparents blamed her in some way. She withdrew, almost like she'd retreated inside herself, and then she moved here. And when I came to see her, after you were born, it was like she was somebody else. All that religion and everything."

"That's the only way I ever knew her."

"I wish you could have known her the way she was back then. She was so full of fun, always smiling, always laughing."

He tried to square that with the mother he had known and could not.

"But it wasn't just the way she changed. I felt guilty."

"Why?"

She bit her lip.

"The creep who did it, the sailor, he asked me to dance first, but I said no. So then he asked her, and I think she felt like she had to, just because I hadn't. And then they got dancing, and he fixated on her. Maybe if I'd said yes, he wouldn't have followed her. I've wondered about that dozens of times."

For a second, he considered telling her what had really happened. But he couldn't, not with his mother here in her coffin.

"Don't beat yourself up over that. There's no way you could have known."

She looked down at her lap.

"That's the worst of it."

"What is?"

"I did know something."

"How?"

"You know where the old Lubec Sardine Company factory used to be? Where the Fisherman's Wharf restaurant is now?"

He shook his head.

"Well, if you were walking downtown from where I lived, the shortest way took you by the factory. Anyway, the factory was shut down, so there wasn't ever anything going on there, but when I walked by earlier that day, I saw two sailors on the wharf. I was a teenager and boy-crazy, so I snuck over to where I could get a better look.

"They had a fishing pole, and the mackerel were running, beating the water into a frenzy the way they do, but they didn't seem to be casting. Then one took a mackerel and sliced its belly open like he was going to clean it, but instead he just tossed it out into the water. Well, of course the gulls came swarming in like they do when there's fish to be had. Then they all took off again, and from the way they did, I could tell the other guy had thrown something. At first, I thought it was just to shoo them off, but then he reached into a bucket and wound up and threw again. I looked out and saw a gull in the water, flapping around like its wing was broken.

"He missed that time, but he must have had a whole bucket of rocks, because he threw again, and this time, I heard the gull squawk. It couldn't fly, and it was trying to swim away, but the tide kept pulling it back in front of the wharf, and he kept throwing rocks. It must have been twenty-five or thirty feet away, but he could really throw. He'd hit it, and the gull would rise up and squawk and scramble a little and try to swim, and he'd hit it again. Then he threw one more, and it gave one final screech and just kind of flattened out on the water."

"God, that's awful. People can be so cruel."

"Isn't that the truth?" She shook her head in revulsion and then continued. "They waited until the current had carried it away, and then the first one slit open another mackerel and threw it out to lure another gull. I was so upset I was trembling. I wanted to yell, but I didn't dare, so I just snuck back to the road and kept going.

"I meant to tell the police. But then I got to town, and I met some friends and got distracted and just kind of forgot about it until we were at the dance. Then this guy comes up and asks me to dance, and he looks really familiar, and I say, 'Did I meet you yesterday?' because they had been in town for a couple of days. And he kind of leers at my chest and says, 'I think I'd remember that,' and then all of a sudden, I recognize him: He's the guy who was throwing the rocks. Just as it hit me, he asked me to dance. I blurted out, 'No, I have to go the ladies' room.' And that's when he asked Clara."

She had been staring straight ahead for the last part of her story, but now she turned toward him again.

"I should have said something. I should have warned her. But I didn't get a chance to talk to her alone before they started dancing, and once they did, he was all over her like white on rice. A friend and I went outside to drink—I mean, we all did during the dances, if anyone had any booze—and then I started dancing with someone else, and . . . well, I never said anything. So that's why I feel like I failed her."

"You're being too hard on yourself."

She squeezed his arm.

"I've told myself that over the years, but I don't believe it. I knew he was bad news. I should have said something, even if I had to do it right in front of him." She was crying now. "I pray that if there's an afterlife, Clara will understand how sorry I am and forgive me."

He gave her a hug.

"I'm sure she will."

The woman said something in response, but though he heard her voice, his mind didn't make sense of the sounds.

All he could think about was Fortin's dog and the way it had flinched and run each time he had raised his arm. Raised his arm the way a person would if he were about to throw something.

CHAPTER 42

HE CIRCLED THE block twice and could see no light from any angle. Drawing the night air deep, he forced himself to exhale in a long, slow, steadying push. If he was going to do it, now was the time. Glancing behind him, he slipped into the side yard. The dog looked expectantly at him, tail thumping the ground.

"You know there's more, don't you, boy?"

He squatted a few feet away and extended the back of his hand, slowly, carefully, keeping his arm just a few inches above the ground. The dog drew back, eyes narrowing.

"C'mere, boy."

Head down, haunches high, it crept forward, sniffing. He turned his hand, and it flinched and then froze, uncertain.

"C'mon."

The creature inched forward again until its nose was almost touching his hand.

He rubbed its snout with his index finger.

"That's right, boy. We're friends, aren't we?"

Now the dog cocked his head sideways, and he scratched behind its ears. He continued stroking the short, coarse fur until the beast had grown accustomed to his touch, then reached his hand slowly to his pocket and withdrew the rest of the roast beef. The dog licked its chops, its tail a frenzy of anticipation.

"Now, c'mon with me."

He led it toward the iron stake that anchored the rope. A few feet away, he unfolded the cellophane, pulled the remaining slices of meat into pieces, and spread them on the ground.

The dog snuffled greedily after the meat, and as it did, he grabbed the rope at about its halfway point and tied it off to the stake.

"There you go, boy."

He eased out of range and around to the rear of the house. The metal storm door was locked. He looked for a key in all the obvious hiding places but found nothing.

You've come this far. You checked the house. You know there's no one there. He's at the Legion. He'll be there till it closes.

Which meant he should have plenty of time. The Legion had to be open until at least ten, and it was barely eight. He had left for Holden Mills immediately after the funeral and had risked a ticket, pushing well above the speed limit to ensure he would make it with time to spare.

He took the big, yellow-handled screwdriver from his shoulder pack and, pulling hard against the door, worked the tip into the space between its inner edge and the frame, pounding it with the heel of his palm. Then he gave a sharp two-handed push.

The latch surrendered with a metallic pop.

The inside door was unlocked. He entered into a kitchen that had room for little more than a sink, a wheezing refrigerator, a small table, and a gas range. He walked over rippled linoleum to the living room that filled the front half of the dwelling.

The shades were drawn, but in the gloom, he could see a reclining chair, a large flat-screen TV, and an old sofa. Reaching into his pocket, he brought out a small flashlight and played its narrow beam across the back of the room. A bathroom with an old white tub and a battered vanity took up the rest of the first floor.

Climbing a narrow staircase, he found himself in a hall with two doorways. He slipped through one into a bedroom. A disheveled bed, visible by the rays of a distant streetlight, was pressed against the wall under the sloping ceiling. He sat on the mattress and dug through the magazines on the nightstand. *Popular Mechanics, Field & Stream, Hustler,* a couple of newspaper sports sections. A dresser opposite the bed had nothing in its three drawers beyond clothing.

A glance out the single window revealed no activity. He crossed the hall into the other room. Its sole piece of furniture was a sturdy wooden chair near the doorway. Several old jackets and two pairs of coveralls hung from hooks on the wall.

In a small closet otherwise stuffed with old blankets, bedding, and towels, he found two boxes, which he dragged over to the chair. He rummaged through the first until he came upon a high-school yearbook. Opening it was like seeing old acquaintances, given the time he had spent already surveying the photographs.

He scrolled through it, looking for notes from classmates. There weren't many. In the front inside cover, someone had written: "To Lester. Four years of Ford, Fortin, Fowler, Frost, all in a roll-call row. Don't let the world tame you."

He riffled the pages, looking for other farewell notes.

"To 'Frowning Les Fortin' from shop, we're leaving this hellhole behind," read one. "To Lester, a guy I never knew very well, but who was super nice to fix my car when it broke down on County Road," scrawled a Linda.

"Too bad about baseball," ended a note a Brad wrote. "You had a hell of an arm. Best pitcher I ever caught."

He put the dusty book down and dug deeper into the box.

There were a number of old report cards showing mostly Cs and an assortment of newspaper clippings tracking the fortunes of the school baseball team.

At the bottom of the pile, a small headline caught his eye.

HOLDEN MILLS BALLPLAYERS ARRESTED AFTER JOY RIDE

Two members of the Holden Mills baseball team were arrested early yesterday morning and charged with grand theft auto and driving under the influence after leading police on a 15-mile chase through back roads in a car they had hot-wired.

Police Sergeant Paul Poulon said the two youths had been drinking heavily.

"They were going in excess of 90 miles per hour, throwing cans out of the car while we pursued them," Poulon said. "We're lucky no one was hurt."

The two teens, whose names are being withheld because they are juveniles, were released on $200 bail after spending a night in jail.

Digging deeper, he found a news brief noting that after a plea bargain, the Aroostook County Juvenile Court had fined the two unnamed miscreants $250 apiece and suspended their licenses for a year. The high-school principal was quoted, saying both had been dropped from the baseball team.

Replacing the yellowed contents of the first box, he began sorting through the second. A layer of auto registrations and insurance-policy papers lay on top, mixed with some old bills and a tax lien from the city.

About halfway down, he found an official-looking folder and opened it to see the Navy's dishonorable discharge after Fortin's rape conviction. Below that was a stack of positive performance reviews, all lauding his work ethic, mastery of all things mechanical, and attention to detail. The one anomaly was a report citing him, along with six other sailors, for drinking on duty while their ship lay in port.

He put the file aside, removed a Navy manual, then cast his flashlight beam down on a thin stack of photographs held together by a frayed rubber band that broke when he rolled it off.

The Statue of Liberty, along with a few other, less easily identifi-able cityscapes, all seen from the water. On the back, he could make out faded longhand notations: Boston, New York, Atlantic City, Virginia Beach, Charleston, Miami, Corpus Christi.

A piece of newspaper was next. He lifted it out to find the top section was folded around several pages of varying typefaces. Small-town papers, they each featured an article about the USS *Saturn* arriving in port.

At the bottom of the pile, he was surprised by the familiar banner of the *Quoddy Tides*, its entire front page devoted to various Downeast Fourth of July celebrations.

He picked up the paper to set it aside, only to find it bulged from the center. Had the little biweekly really been such a thick paper in those days?

As he turned it over, a corner projecting at an incongruous angle caught his eye. Opening the newspaper at its fold, he stared at a yellowed panel of newsprint.

GIRL, 15, REPORTS RAPE

So he had kept that too, the record of his own undoing there in four spare words.

But fifteen? His mother had been seventeen.

He held the story up, squinting at the yellowed page. "A 15-year-old Norfolk girl told police she was raped in Virginia Beach by a man who accosted her at knifepoint after a bonfire party."

He picked up the sheet of newsprint beneath and brought it closer to his beam.

BRUNSWICK TEEN SLAIN

A 16-year-old Brunswick, Georgia, girl was found dead yesterday, less than a mile from the spot where a group of high-school youths had been gathered for a nighttime beach party. The girl's throat had been cut with a sharp blade, according to police detective Larry Duffen, who said that her body was just several hundred yards from the path to Fairmont Beach.

Duffen said the body was positively identified yesterday as that of Darlene Baskin, a junior at Brunswick High School.

"From the evidence, it appears that the victim was attacked by someone who intended to sexually assault her," said Duffen, who added that the crime scene showed indications of a brief but intense struggle.

Police have no immediate suspects, though yesterday a law-enforcement task force was interviewing youths who attended the Thursday-night bonfire, which went on into the early morning hours.

Duffen said that though police had not recovered
the murder weapon, the wound it had left on the victim indicated a blade of the sort . . .

The next few lines had faded almost to illegibility.

He brought the yellowed print closer to his face and focused his
light on the spot. As he did, he sensed a slight change in the shadows
just beyond the reach of his beam.

CHAPTER 43

INSTINCT SENT HIM dodging right, even as he brought his left arm up to shield his head.

But not fast enough. His arm absorbed some of the blow, but whatever it was kept coming, slamming his temple hard enough to snap his head back.

Reality exploded in a blinding brisance of pain.

Staggering sideways, he saw that it was a bat—a bat that was coming at him again, slicing downward.

Then his leg was on fire with agony.

He lurched away. He was against the wall now, trying to find sight, balance, and reflexes in the drunken, disordered world of pain.

He pushed hard off the wall, but not in time. The bat thudded into his ribs, followed by a jab of pain so fierce it felt as though a dagger had been run through his side.

Falling, falling. He had to get up. Had to.

He rolled left. The bat thudded just behind him, its impact reverberating through the floor. He pushed off his knees, made it to his feet, gasping for air.

Concentrate. He had to breathe, to get beyond the agony, to clear his head.

The bat drew back, waiting, feinting. One more and he'd collapse. And then he'd be gone. It struck him that this was what it was like for a fighter who gets stunned by a punch and finds himself half a second behind in those frantic, fractured moments as the succeeding blows slam home. A fighter who can never recover and is soon knocked out. Who never knows what happened to him.

Ten seconds. That was all he needed. Ten seconds for the fog to lift, for his reflexes to return.

"You did it, you son of a bitch. She didn't lie. You did it, just like she said. You raped her."

The words came out slurred and desperate, but they provoked a reply.

"You can't rape a whore."

"You killed the other girl. She fought back, so you killed her."

"Yeah, and I should've killed the Lubec bitch too. Then she never would've grunted you out. I knew you'd be back."

"I knew you were lying. That's why I came back." He pawed at the blood streaming into his eye. "Now I know I'm right." The chair. He was in front of it.

"Fat lot of good it'll do you. Our little secret's gonna die with you, the punk I caught robbing my house. The punk who attacked me and got a whole lot more than he bargained for."

Through clearing vision, he could see the cocked bat start to move. Grabbing the chair with both hands, he pivoted and swung it in front of him. There was a sharp sound of wood on wood, then a whoosh as the bat swept by, inches from his face.

Breathe, breathe.

He scrambled through the doorway and into the hall.

He heard the bat thud into the doorframe.

Now. Now. Attack.

He pushed off the opposite wall and sent his right fist into Fortin's face.

"Aggghhh."

Blood gushed from the man's nose. He drove his other fist into the same spot and saw one of Fortin's hands fly up. Propelled by instinct, he grabbed the bat, twisted, and smashed an elbow into Fortin's head. He wrenched again. The bat came free. He fixed a tight grip on the handle and took a step. The bat swung into Fortin's shoulder with a hard impact that brought a roar of pain.

A roar that fed the rage building inside him.

Now Fortin stood in front of him, dripping blood, breathing hard, eyeing him warily, twitching as though ready to dodge.

The bat swung again, but as it did, the man stepped forward, too close for the bat's barrel to catch him, his right arm angling in. Dan saw the glint of the knife in his hand and felt the blade slice into his left arm.

But the wound registered only in a distant way, as pain that fed and focused the fury that possessed him.

Fortin feinted, then brought the knife arcing at him again.

He pulled back, seeing, sensing, knowing that the blade's sweep would be short. At the precise moment it passed, he swung. The bat's blow sent Fortin tumbling to the floor, the knife clattering across the room. In a second, it was in his grasp, and he thudded down onto the prostrate form.

The man struggled to rise.

Dan pushed the knife point against his neck and held it there with both hands. "Move and you die."

Fortin lay back. "Now you see what it's like. Now you know. You can't escape it. It's who you are." The words were low, hateful, mocking.

Dan burned with the urge to plunge the knife down and end that loathsome voice.

"One more word, and I swear, I'll fucking kill you."

"Do it. It's who you are. We both know it. It's who you fucking are."

CHAPTER 44

A HEAVY FOG blanketed Eastport, a fog that cleared only to a wet smear under the thumping of the truck's windshield wipers as Griff drove along Water Street.

"Man, this sucks. Rain all day, fog all night."

"It's Maine, dude. You love Maine, remember?"

"Not this part. I've got a ton of deliveries tomorrow, and Susan wants to go to dinner to some new place in Pembroke. I hope to hell it clears."

Sonny blew a plume of cigarette smoke toward the thin slice of open window.

"I hope it hangs. Then the old man won't want to be on the water at the crack of fucking dawn."

He had swung by Sonny's when he'd gotten done with the Thursday oil route, mostly to avoid the monotony of another night at home. Weekend nights, he and Susan were most always together, and he was with her on weekdays when there was a basketball game or something else of civic note. But the other nights, he had to fend for himself, because she, having acceded to her parents' wishes and enrolled at the community college in Calais, had schoolwork. In two years, she'd have an associate's degree and credits she could transfer to the state university system.

"Just in case you change your mind and decide to go to UMaine," her mother had said in a voice Susan mimicked perfectly.

"In case you decide to dump me, she means."

She squeezed his hand.

"It's only two years, Griff. Then whatever I do, they can't complain."

Even if you marry me? he'd wanted to ask. After all, they were established enough as a couple now that townsfolk who made other people's business their own were speculating that wedding bells were coming, sooner or later. "Sooner, if they're not careful," some of the rakish types joked, something he knew because his mother had relayed as much, along with the admonition that she hoped they were being careful.

Her parents also must know they were sleeping together. Or maybe they preferred not to think about it. Still, they wanted her to keep her options open, which was why she drove to Calais four days a week in the used Ford Focus her folks had bought her as an inducement—"my bribe ride," she called it—and studied most school nights.

He missed her on the nights they weren't together, but she was right; two years wasn't that long. He could find things to do, even if it was just hanging with Sonny.

"Don't know about you, but I'm thirsty."

"Damn straight."

He swung the truck into Stanhope's and, since Sonny had bought the last time, got out and walked across the puddled parking lot and into the store.

"How you doing, Griff?" said Peter McKinney, who was standing behind the counter in a Red Sox baseball cap, faded jeans, and a blue T-shirt with a cartoon of a beer-drinking beach boy eyeing a buxom, micro-bikinied blonde, with a caption that read, "You know what would look good on you? Me!"

Griff put a six-pack of Heineken bottles and two bags of barbecue potato chips on the counter.

"Better soon."

"You drinking that alone, or is Sonny with you?"

"The two of us."

"Hey, just so's you know, Dan Winters is back."

"Yeah, I heard his mother died. The loony church lady."

"Let's hope that's the only reason." McKinney slid the beer into a paper bag.

"Whaddya mean?"

"I gave him a ride in from Perry the other day. He was going on about you and Sonny."

"Like what?"

McKinney frowned and pushed his lips from one side of his jaw to the other.

"How you're a fucking jerk who started things when you had your dust-up, but he was the one who had pay for it. And how Sonny's an asshole. Something like that."

Griff waited for McKinney to slide the bag of beer and chips his way, something he seemed to be in no hurry to do.

"So anyway, just a word to the wise."

"Thanks."

"What are you two doing tonight? Going to the party at Gleason's?"

Griff shook his head.

"Nah. Not in this fog."

"So where you headed?"

"I don't know. Maybe take these green soldiers up to the war memorial and give 'em a proper send-off."

McKinney finally slid the bag of beer across the counter to him.

"Where's Susan?"

"She's got homework."

"She'll be jealous that you're up there with Sonny. You'll have to make her pussycat purr to set things rights. But I suppose you're good at that."

Griff forced a wan smile.

"What she don't know won't hurt her," he returned and instantly felt like an idiot for saying it. "Anyway, catch you later."

McKinney nodded.

"Later."

"What took you so long?" Sonny said when he was back in the truck.

"McKinney wouldn't shut up. Kinda holding the beer hostage, so I had to listen."

"What's on his mind?"

"He says Winters is in town."

Sonny opened a bottle of Heineken and handed it to Griff as he drove up Water Street, then popped the cap on another, tilted the beer back, and belched.

"Yeah?"

"Pete gave him a ride into town the other day. Says Winters was talking trash about us."

"Like what?" Sonny said, head turning toward him.

"How I started it, but he had to pay. And how you're an asshole."

The drove in silence for a moment, then Sonny spoke again.

"You still got your gun, right?"

"It's under the seat."

"So, the bonfire at Gleason's?"

"Not in this fog."

"Breakwater, then?"

"Nah. I don't feel like shooting the shit with anybody tonight."

"You could just head back to the old folks' home."

Ignoring him, Griff turned left on High Street and started down through the cemetery, which lay on both sides of the road.

"Let's go to the war memorial and remember Eastport's heroes with a couple of these green soldiers," he said, tipping his beer.

It was somewhere they could lay low without admitting that was their intent. To each other or themselves.

"That way, if something happens, nobody can ever say we went looking for him."

"Suits me," Sonny said.

CHAPTER 45

DAN DROVE SLOWLY down onto the breakwater, peering through the mist at the various vehicles parked there, looking for Susan's family Subaru or a pickup like the one he remembered Kimball driving during high school. Those two together . . .

And if they were a thing, they were no doubt sleeping together. That would be the case even if this weren't Eastport.

It said something about the way time is experienced in places with limited possibilities, places where people and prospects circle endlessly back upon themselves in the eddies of small-town life. In Portland or Bangor, or even Augusta or Brunswick or Bath, if a girl disliked an asshole like Kimball, their lives would be lived far enough apart that she'd continue disliking him.

But not here. Here, there was no separation. You saw the same people day after day, time after time. And when you didn't see them, you heard about them. So maybe new moments, new memories, took the edge off the old ones, until they didn't matter any longer.

Still, even for Eastport, this was strange. As far as the town knew, he and Kimball had mixed it up because Griff had called Susan a slut. And now the two of them were together, and he, the one who had supposedly stuck up for her, had gone away for it. Except that wasn't what really happened. Still, it was small-town strange.

Well, it was what it was, and it didn't concern him any longer. He just wanted to find Griff, make it clear that as far as he was concerned, the past was the past. Then he'd visit his mother's grave in the morning and leave Eastport in the rearview mirror. Anything else that needed to be done could be done by phone.

He was approaching the far end of the breakwater's L and started a sweeping U-turn.

His left arm—his swollen, knife-sliced arm—ached so badly that he had to do it all with his right, which meant rotating the steering wheel almost fully around and then letting go and making a quick grab of the right side to complete the spin.

The breakwater didn't contain any vehicles that looked like theirs—not on the first swing he did or on a subsequent one after driving around town.

So who'd know? He couldn't exactly go to Kimball's. Or to Susan's.

Then it hit him. McKinney, the slumpy, small-town fuckwit who had given him a ride in from Perry. He sat behind the convenience-store counter collecting gossip and keeping track of the town's coming and goings most every night. If anyone had a notion about where to find Griff, it would be McKinney.

He wheeled off the breakwater and headed toward the convenience store where McKinney had worked probably from the time he graduated from high school and would no doubt stay until he retired. Or found some way to bang out on long-term disability.

How had they parted? No angry words. Not really. He'd just gotten out of the car.

McKinney was sitting there behind the counter when he came in.

"Hey," Dan said as he headed toward the drinks cooler. He grabbed two Red Bulls, then found a pack of Fig Newtons and two Snickers bars and put it all on the counter.

"Now there's a dinner for you."

He forced a laugh.

"Long drive tomorrow."

He felt McKinney looking him over and knew what was coming, but he'd given this some thought and was ready for it.

"What the hell happened to you?"

"I got mugged."

"Jesus. Who did it?"

"They didn't give me their name."

"Around here?"

"Close enough," he answered, and then, before McKinney could ask his next question, he added, "Hey, have you seen Kimball tonight?"

"He was in for some beer."

"Was he heading up to Gleason's?"

McKinney shook his head.

"I think he said he was having an early night. You check the breakwater?"

"Twice."

He picked his bag up and turned toward the door.

"You could try the war memorial, up at the head of the cemetery. Somebody I talked to tonight mentioned going there. Mighta been him."

CHAPTER 46

"I SAW DAN WINTERS the other night."

Susan looked up from the history text she was studying as her mother made supper.

"Where?"

"At Grantley's Funeral Home."

"What was he doing there?"

"His mother died."

"Oh my God, when?"

"Three or four days ago."

"How?"

"She was in an accident, up in Robbinston. The car she was driving skidded off the road and down an embankment. Mrs. Holmes asked me to take her to the funeral home for visiting hours. I guess Mrs. Winters used to come over and cook for her."

"What'd he say?"

"Not much." Mrs. Jameison opened the oven door and checked on the meatloaf. "There was quite a crowd. I only saw him for a minute."

"How was he?"

"Like you'd expect. Quiet, maybe even a little stunned. He asked about you."

"What about me?"

"Just what you were doing. He seemed surprised you weren't at UMaine. He's at Bates now."

Susan sighed theatrically. So this was the point of the whole thing? That even Dan Winters, a poor kid raised by a single mother, a guy who had been sent away to reform school, thought she should be at a four-year college?

"I hope you told him to mind his own business."

"Wouldn't that have been polite, at his mother's funeral?"

"So what did you say?"

"I said you were going to the community college."

"I hope that was okay with him—in his new job as guidance counselor, I mean."

"Oh, Susan."

"So that's all?"

Mrs. Jameison bit her lip.

"I said you were going pretty steady with Griff."

Susan snapped her book closed and stood up.

"Oh my God, Mom, tell me you didn't! You know what he did to Griff."

"I know, honey, but it slipped my mind. I hadn't thought about it in ages." Mrs. Jameison turned from the stove to face her daughter. "Does it really matter?"

"Does it really matter that you told a guy who's so crazy that he attacked Griff for making a sarcastic remark about me, which he didn't even mean, that I'm now going out with him?"

When a long moment had passed without a reply, Susan asked, "Well, what did he say?"

"Not much. He seemed surprised."

"Surprised how?"

"Just . . . surprised." She pursed her lips. "You don't think he'd do something?"

"You don't know him. Tell me exactly what he said."

"He said, 'Susan, with Griff? Wow.' Something like that."

"Nothing else?"

"He said he and Griff hadn't had any problems."

Susan made an incredulous face.

"Oh really? Then how did Griff end up in the hospital?"

"Ongoing problems, I mean. He said Griff had started the whole thing that day."

"Mom, why did that even come up?"

"Because I said I liked Griff and that I wished they hadn't had problems."

Susan was on her feet now. She took her coat from the closet and put it on.

"Where are you going?"

"I'm going to find Griff."

"Can't it wait?"

"I don't know, Mom. I just don't know."

CHAPTER 47

A NIMBUS OF light brightened the fog.

"Somebody's coming."

Griff's throat tightened. Once he'd driven down the cemetery road and parked up behind the nub of the rise, his sense of menace had faded.

But now . . .

A car emerged from the mist. They watched it nose through the fog toward the memorial and then up beyond the boulder, swinging right, toward them.

When its headlights hit the truck, it stopped. The lights went off. The door opened.

"Holy fuck, it's him," Sonny said. "It's really him."

Winters was here.

Jesus. So it was really going to happen. Just like in his dreams.

Except for real this time.

He pulled the gun out from its sweatshirt nest beneath the seat, unholstered it, pushed the magazine in till it clicked, shucked a bullet into the chamber, flipped the safety off.

"Stay by the truck," Sonny said. "When he starts coming, I'll hit the lights. It's self-defense, Griff. I'll swear to it."

He was shaking. He squeezed hard on the pistol grip to steady himself.

You can do this. You can do it. Just do what you've done a hundred times before.

Support.

Sight.

Squeeze.

CHAPTER 48

GRIFF WASN'T AT home, and his mother had no idea where he'd gone.

"He doesn't tell me his plans, Susan. I'm just the cook. And the maid. And the laundry service. Did you try his phone?"

"Yeah. But you know how reception is on nights like this."

"Everything okay?"

She nodded. "I just wanted to see him for a minute."

"Any message?"

"No, just ask him to call me."

There was a party in Perry, but she doubted Griff would go there. More likely he'd be riding around with Sonny. The thought made her grimace.

From Water Street, the breakwater looked empty, though it was too foggy to tell for certain. She drove its length. His pickup wasn't there.

Suddenly it struck her where they'd be. She gunned the car up Adams Street toward the cemetery.

CHAPTER 49

WAVES OF NAUSEA rose from his gut.

He had to stop shaking.

He gripped the gun tighter, took a deep breath and held it.

You can do this. Just like you're shooting bottles.

Support.

Sight.

Squeeze.

Susan slammed the car into park and leapt out.

There was Griff's pickup—and him beside it. Even in the gloom, she could tell instantly, instinctively, that it was him.

Fifty feet away, the other figure—Dan, it had to be Dan—took a step toward him.

Winters had something in his hand. A bat. No, too thin. Maybe a piece of pipe.

He clenched his jaw to stop his teeth from chattering.

It's just you and him now.

You can do this.

You know you can.

Support.

Sight.

Squeeze.

He's crazy and he's coming after you.

You can do this.

You have to.

It's just you and him.

The fear began to fade.

Light flooded the clearing, startling Susan and blinding her for a second.

Headlights.

From the pickup.

But who had . . .

It couldn't be Griff.

He was standing there, holding something.

Pointing something.

A gun.

"Griff! No, no, no. Oh God, *no!*"

She was running now.

Griff was too far away, but Dan, Dan was closer. She had to get to him.

CHAPTER 50

HE FELT THE familiar mass of the pistol, the steadying presence of his left hand, saw the front sight come level in the notch of the rear. Winters took another step.

Suddenly, he was awash in light.

Don't jerk the trigger. Squeeze it—squeeze it, just like you always do.

His whole being was focused now.

"Griff! No, no, no. Oh God, *no!*"

That voice, the figure running toward Winters, in front of him now.

It was Susan.

He felt the pistol buck in his hand. It had fired, fired even as his brain had sent a frantic message to stop the support, sight, squeeze sequence his muscle memory knew so well.

Fired because part of him, the part that was purpose forged in fear, had stayed fixed on supporting, sighting, squeezing, even as the part that was consciousness and not instinct had screamed to jerk the gun aside.

Susan and Winters lay on the ground. He took one step toward them, then another.

One squeeze of the finger, one bullet. Had it changed everything?

Now Sonny was beside him.

"Oh fuck. Fuck, fuck, fuck."

CHAPTER 51

THE PISTOL'S RETORT rang in his ears. Something—someone—tumbled into him.

He felt himself hit the ground, felt a searing pain explode in his chest.

My God, Kimball shot me. The fucker shot me.

So this is what it feels like. This is it.

No, no—you've felt that pain before.

It was his injured ribs, screaming in sharp, thudding agony under Susan's weight. It was Susan. He knew that. He had only half seen her, but his brain had processed the sound of her voice. She lay across him, sobbing.

"Are you all right?" he said. He brought his free arm to her face. "Susan, are you all right?"

She lifted her head for a second, then let it fall back.

"I . . . I think so. Oh my God. I heard the bullet. I heard it go by. Oh my God."

She broke into a sob, then caught herself again.

"Dan, why are you doing this?"

"Doing what? I just wanted to tell him it's over and done with. And the fucking idiot tries to shoot me."

Griff saw the dark bodies start to untangle, saw Susan lift herself to her hands and knees and then stand up. Now Winters began to move.

"Susan."

"Griff, put the gun down."

"Susan, are you okay?"

"Yes, I'm okay. Put the gun down, Griff."

He kept it at waist level, barrel pointing ahead, and walked forward. Winters raised himself to a sitting position, his right leg splayed out to his side like a bird's broken wing.

"He wants to tell you something, Griff. That's why he's here. Tell him, Dan."

He looked at Griff, then at the gun.

"The stuff between us—it's done. With me, anyway."

Susan's arm was on Griff's now.

"Griff, put the gun down. Please. For me. Put it down."

"It's bullshit, Griff. He's been looking for you. He came here to get you."

Susan whirled to face Sonny, who had come up from behind Griff.

"Sonny, would you shut up? Would you just shut the fuck up?"

Sonny took a step toward Winters.

"Easy to say it's done when you're staring at the barrel of a gun, isn't it, you fucking son of a crazy raped bitch."

Winters turned toward Sonny and stared for a long moment. "Yeah, she was raped. Raped by someone who threatened to kill her. And yeah, maybe it threw her off. But what's your excuse, Beal? What the fuck is your excuse for being such a goddamn worthless piece of shit?"

Griff looked from Winters to Susan to Sonny. He lowered the pistol.

"Sonny, do like Susan said. Shut up. Just shut up."

CHAPTER 52

HE STOOD FOR a moment reading the headstone, then took another small step, leaning heavily on the cane and bracing for the pain he knew would come. The only time it had been absent was in the frantic aftermath of the fight with Fortin and then only until the adrenaline had worn off.

Thankfully, it had sent enough energy pumping through him to keep his head clear, his body functioning. But even then, as he lay on top of Fortin, pressing the knife to his throat, he had known his time and energy were limited and ebbing.

"Do it. It's who you are. We both know it. It's who you fucking are."

He had raised himself on his injured arm and sent his right elbow smashing hard into Fortin's face. Then he had rolled, keeping the knife above him, staggered to his feet, and stumbled down the stairs.

The man would have a gun. He would have a gun. He had to move, move fast, before he could retrieve it.

He was moving as fast as he could, but now time seemed to slow. He reached for the door with his injured arm and tried to turn the knob, but his hand, slick with blood and weak, couldn't get the necessary grip. With his right hand, he moved the knife down and gripped it between his knees, then used his good hand to pull the door in and open.

Knife back in his right, he slammed through the metal outer door.

When he did, the dog rose and strained against his foreshortened rope, looking at him eagerly. The image came back again of the way the beast had scurried away when he'd raised his arm.

Fuck. Fuck. Fuck.

How fast could Fortin move?

He knelt beside the dog and grabbed the rope and lashed at it with the knife. One strand parted, and then another with a second slash, and then a third.

"Okay, boy, that's all I can do."

He pushed himself back to his feet and ran to the road, lurching from side to side to present a more difficult target. Now he had a tree between him and the house and now another.

He kept loping.

The ground was coming up at him, meeting his feet before they were ready, and he stumbled and went into slow motion again, and he couldn't get an arm up in time to protect his head, and it smashed into the graveled side of the road.

Fuck.

He had to get up.

He did.

He staggered on, lurched through a backyard and out onto another street.

His right hand was empty. He had lost the knife. He had no weapon.

But there were lights ahead, green and yellow. Store lights. He had to keep going. Had to. He fixated on the lights.

Now he was at a glass door. He steadied himself against it, then pushed the door open.

A thirty-something woman looked up from the counter.

"Call the police. Call the police," he said—and collapsed on the floor.

An ambulance had taken him to the emergency room, where they had stitched him up, bandaged his arm, transfused some blood, checked for a concussion, and X-rayed and then bound his ribs. He had spent the night there.

The local police had visited the next morning and then, when the attending physician said he was well enough to leave, had transported him to the police station, where he had waited half an hour in an airless interrogation room before a State Police detective came in.

Fit as a Marine, the uniformed officer looked at him with a gray-eyed squint.

"So before we get into details, I want to be sure we understand each other. You are telling me you got into this fight after breaking into somebody's house, and now you say he's a murderer?"

"Yes."

"You know breaking and entering is a crime?"

"Yeah."

"Do you want a lawyer present?"

"I'd rather just tell you the story."

The detective arched his eyebrows.

"I need to advise you that if you incriminate yourself—which seems pretty likely, given what you've already told me—you could be arrested. And what you've said could be used against you."

"I know."

"And you still don't want a lawyer?"

"I'll take my chances."

The man pulled a digital recorder from his pocket, pressed a button, and put it on the table.

"Okay. So tell me what happened."

"I should start by saying that the man who lives there raped my mother back when she was in high school. And that I'm his son."

If his interrogator felt any surprise, he didn't betray it.

"Can you prove that?"

"He went to prison for the rape. The other, not without a DNA test. But I know it's true. So did he."

"What's his name again?"

"Lester Fortin."

"F-O-R-T-I-N?"

"Yup."

He opened the door and leaned into the hall.

"Debbie, can you run Lester Fortin for me?"

He turned back to Dan.

"What's your mother's name?"

"Clara Winters. But she's dead."

"Not of foul play?"

"No. A car accident."

The detective nodded.

"Okay. Give me a minute."

It was fifteen minutes before he returned, a computer printout in one hand, a can of orange juice in the other.

"You thirsty?"

"Thanks."

He slid the can across the table.

"Let's start this again, Dan. I'm Brian Chadwick. Just take your time, and tell me your story."

For the next half an hour, Chadwick listened as he spoke of his adolescent questions, of his discovery of the metal box in the attic, of the statement inside, of his meeting with Fortin and the story he had told about his mother. Of the woman at the funeral, of breaking into Fortin's house and finding the old newspaper stories, of the fight.

"Did you take the clippings?"

He shook his head.

"I didn't have time. I was looking at them when he jumped me."

"Okay. Hang on."

Again, he opened the door.

"Debbie, can you get the DA on the line?"

"This is a tough one, Dan," Chadwick said, sitting back down. "Even if we had the clippings, it wouldn't really prove anything. Having newspaper stories about a murder doesn't make you a murderer. It might suggest something to a jury, but it's totally circumstantial, as the defense would remind them again and again. And if Fortin has a brain in his head, he's already gotten rid of them. Plus, the cases themselves are old. The statute of limitations will have run out on everything except for the murder. You remember the name?"

"It was Baskin. Darlene Baskin. From Brunswick, Georgia."

"And the year?"

"I didn't see that, but if it was the same summer, it would have been twenty years ago."

"All right, let me see what I can find. You need anything?"

"Maybe something to read."

"I'll have Debbie bring you some magazines from the squad room."

He had read three articles in a month-old *Sports Illustrated* before the door opened again.

"The DA will be here in an hour. Meanwhile, we called Georgia. They do have an unsolved by the name of Baskin, from that time. No good evidence. No weapon, no prints, no DNA. Nothing, really, but the body. And now it's two decades old. So here's the issue. The DA wants to bring Fortin in for questioning, and we're going to ask a judge for a search warrant. But chances are we won't find much, and he's obviously not going to confess. That means the case would pretty much come down to you."

"To me?"

"To him telling you that he did it. It could be that's everything we'd have to hang this on. You're sure of what he said?"

"It's burned into my brain. I said that he'd killed the other girl because she fought back, and he said, 'Yeah, and I should've killed the Lubec bitch, too. Then she never would've grunted you out."

His gaze set on the ceiling, Chadwick mulled that over for a minute.

"It's something, but it's not a lot. We'd pretty much have to convince the jury with your testimony alone. You couldn't waver even a little. If they could get you to vary it by even a word or two, that would blow a big hole in our case. And there'd be news coverage, lots of it. Not just in Maine. All over the country. Everybody'd know about it."

He thought of his friends at Bates, of the murmur that would run through campus as word spread. He'd spent his time there side-stepping questions about his past, giving his history in a vague way that omitted the long months in reform school.

But that was nothing compared to what they'd know now. The son of a rapist. Something he couldn't be blamed for but which would still change everything.

Hannah would say it didn't matter, that it had nothing to do with him, with who he was. But it did, of course. Wouldn't she—wouldn't any girl her age—decide that it was just too much to deal with?

He could leave Bates. He could go to the Midwest, or California, even, after the trial and seek refuge in the anonymity of a large university. Would it follow him there? Ten years from now, when he met someone, would they frown in puzzlement and ask themselves—or, worse, him—where they had heard his name before? How would they act as the details came trickling back from the watershed of memory?

He looked at Chadwick.

"There's something else. I did a year in juvie—the Long Creek Center."

"For what?"

And so he told that story too.

"Would that hurt the case?"

"Some. They'd certainly use it to go after your credibility. We'll have to see what the DA thinks. But even if he wants to go forward, you have to decide if you do."

"What would you do?"

"I don't think I'd have the same choice to make."

"Why's that?"

"Because I would have killed the bastard. So I'd have to tell my story to defend myself in court."

Chadwick appraised him for a moment.

"Cunning SOB, though. He made the right bet."

"Huh?"

"Challenging you to kill him. He made a judgment you weren't like him, despite what he may have said to you. He knew it'd make you stop."

Dan thought of the moment—of the murderous rage, of the knife in his hand and Fortin pinned beneath him. And of how his mother's voice had come to him amid the furious roar in his head.

"A boy with your talents can be anything you want to be. It's all up to you."

"If so, he took a big gamble. It was close."

"Most life-or-death moments are."

Taking a long last look, he traced his fingers over the top of the granite headstone, then turned and limped back to the car.

CHAPTER 53

RAIN WAS BLOWING in off the St. Croix River, the first small drops hitting her face as she hurried along the path to the campus parking lot.

"Susan."

He was waiting there by her car.

They hadn't spoken since that night. For the first week, when he'd tried her every day, hearing his ring tone had triggered a jolt of longing. But she had been resolute about letting it go to voicemail—and then about deleting the message, unheard.

When her mother said he'd called the house, she'd said to tell him she was away for a few days if he called back.

"I'm not going to lie to him, Susan."

"Then say I need some time to think about things. That's the truth."

"I wish you'd tell me what happened."

"I'm too upset to talk about it."

"He didn't hit you, did he?"

She thought for a half-second of the sound of the bullet, inches from her ear.

"No."

"Is there someone else?"

"Mom, could you please just tell him what I said?"

She stopped. He was standing near the driver's side of the Focus. To get in, she would have to step around him.

"Susan, I have to talk to you."

"I'm sorry, Griff. There's nothing you could say that would change anything."

"But we . . . we were so great together. We belong together."

"I thought so. But not anymore."

"Please, Susan." He put his hand on her shoulder, but she felt it only in an abstract way, a way that didn't seem at all connected to him.

"Griff, you had a gun. You shot at him."

"But nobody got hurt, because of you. I know how much I owe you. I'll never forget it. Never. If you could just forgive me . . ."

She wiped some rain from her forehead and looked directly into his eyes.

"It's not a matter of me forgiving you and everything just going back to the way it was, Griff. I have no idea who you really are. If someone had told me you had a gun and you were planning on shooting him, I would have said, *No way—not in a million years.*"

"I wasn't planning on shooting him. I was trying to avoid him. That's why we were there. But when he showed up, I thought he was coming after me. I mean, what was I supposed to think? He must have looked all over to find us there. How would he even know about that spot?"

She felt a pang of guilt about the lie she had told him. But that didn't, that couldn't, excuse what he had done.

"Griff, he lives—lived—in the North End. He probably walked through there to get to school."

"But why would he ever think I'd be there?"

"It doesn't matter. He was coming to tell you it was all over and done with."

"But I didn't know that, Susan. You know what he did last time."

"You didn't know, because you shot before he had a chance to say anything. You're lucky he's not dead."

"I know. I know. You saved him. You saved me. It could have been so awful. But it wasn't, because of you. In a way, it's like nothing even happened."

The wind was coming in gusts now, bringing thickening rain.

"Everything happened, Griff. Everything. I heard the bullet go by my ear. I mean, I could hear it splitting the air. It was that close."

"I tried to jerk my hand up when I saw you. I'd rather die than hurt you, Susan. Tell me you believe that."

"I do believe that, Griff. I do. But it doesn't matter. I feel like you're a stranger. Like the guy I thought I knew better than I've ever known anyone, the guy I loved, has actually been someone else the whole time."

Like the character in that movie you like so much, she almost said, but by the time the name *Martin Guerre* came to her, she had decided against it, because that analogy, any analogy, would sound false compared to what she felt.

He started to speak again, but she interrupted with the question that had pushed its way into her mind.

"Sonny told you to get the gun, didn't he?"

He was silent for a few seconds, then shook his head.

"Not really."

"Not really? What's that mean, Griff?"

"It means I'm trying to be honest, trying to remember. Trying to tell you the truth. He might have mentioned it, but I would have gotten one anyway. Winters is crazy."

"Sonny's the one who's crazy. But you don't see that. You never have."

"I'll quit hanging around with him. I'll never speak to him again, I swear to God. Just give me another chance. Give us another chance."

She shook her head.

"I'd be like a battered wife, always worried, always scared."

"Scared of what? Not of me."

"Scared I didn't know what you might do."

"Nothing like that will ever happen again. I promise." His voice broke, and despite the rain, she could see he was crying. "It will be the way it was."

"I wish it could be, Griff. I've lain there night after night, wishing that. But there's a whole other side to you that I don't know. And I can't love someone I don't know."

"I'll do anything."

"Then find yourself, Griff. Figure out who you really are. But don't do it for me. It's too late for that. Do it for yourself."

"I will. But you have to give me another chance. You have to."

The rain was slanting in hard off the river now, pelting their faces. Her hair was plastered to her head, and her Gap zip-up was soaked, but she stood there silently, resolved not to speak again nor to move until he did.

He started to say something, then, choking back a sob, put his hand on her arm. He gave it a gentle squeeze and turned and walked back to his truck.

She watched as he drove away. Only when the pickup had disappeared did she finally unlock the car and get in.

CHAPTER 54

THE POLICE CRUISER slowed and pulled up next to him as he got out of his pickup. The driver's window slid down, and Mel Tolland ducked to lean his head out.

"Hey, Griff."

"Hi."

"Gotta minute?"

Tolland was an avuncular presence to many of the high-school athletes because he sometimes drove members of the various teams to away games when a school bus and driver weren't to be had. As police chief, Tolland had been sympathetic after Griff's fight with Winters. Griff nodded with what he hoped was nonchalance.

"Sure."

"Why don't we take a ride?"

Griff settled in on the passenger's side. The car carried the strong fake-pine scent of the cardboard air freshener that hung from the mirror, and after a half-dozen breaths, he could feel a boil of nausea rising in his gut.

"Mind if I crack the window?"

"You're not a prisoner, Griff. If you were, you'd be in the back."

Tolland headed up High Street past the high school and then out through the cemetery, taking a right on Clark Street. He turned down a dead-end road, pulled to the shoulder in a spot with a sweeping view of the bay, and shut the engine off.

"I don't imagine you want anybody seeing you with the chief of police."

"I don't mind."

"Well, it's a nice view out here anyway," the chief said, shifting his angular frame in the seat. He appraised his passenger for a moment and then chuckled.

"No offense, Griff, but you look like five miles of bad road."

"I feel like ten."

His head was pounding, and though he had already drunk two big bottles of seltzer, his mouth was desert dry.

Sinking into despair after his plea to Susan, he had driven through Calais and out Route 9. He had thought about just keeping on, through the afternoon and evening and night, into the next day and beyond.

Then second thoughts had set in. Where would he go? What would he do? It wasn't that he wanted to be somewhere else. He didn't want to be anywhere at all, except with her. Driving wouldn't cure that.

So he had stopped at a convenience store in Baring, where his fake ID passed the bored clerk's cursory inspection.

"You like that shit?" he said, looking at the six-pack of Colt 45 Griff set on the counter.

"Does the job."

He opened a can and drank deep and had more as he wound his way east on forested roads, tracing a route marked only in memory back toward the lake.

He stopped at Bishop's Field, gone-wild farmland used for parking by those who came to swim at the small beach across the road. He'd finished his first beer by then. He drank another, staring out across the slate-gray water.

He felt a sudden urge to leave and so drove back to Perry Corner and then to Gleason's Cove, where he pulled into a remote spot and drank another can, then opened a fourth.

There was no hope he and Susan would get back together, and he wondered if he would ever escape the desolation her loss had created. He guzzled the rest of that can and then closed his eyes and refused to let any thought take shape. This was how it must be to be dead. No, it couldn't be, because he was thinking. He forced even that thin shoot of contemplation from his mind.

When he woke up, the sun was rising over Deer Island, Canada.

"I got kind of drunk last night. At Gleason's."

Might as well be honest about that; as long as the liquor hadn't come from his jurisdiction, Tolland wouldn't care. "I didn't drive. I slept in the truck."

"No wonder you're a mess. Something wrong?"

"Susan and I broke up."

Tolland frowned.

"Sorry to hear that. You two seemed like the real deal. You okay?"

"It's pretty tough."

"Time has a way of making things better."

"I don't see how it could."

"Trust me, it does."

He looked down at his knees rather than replying.

Tolland's dark eyebrows became punctuation points of concern.

"You're not thinking of doing anything drastic?"

"Nothing seems drastic right now."

"People care about you, Griff."

"Not her. Not anymore. And she's all I can think about."

The chief worried his lips.

"No chance of putting it back together? Sometimes a dozen roses and an apology will do a world of good."

"I've tried. She's done."

"Well, again, I'm sorry, Griff. I really am. I want you to promise me you'll talk to someone if you get to thinking you should just end it all. Me, if you don't have anybody else."

When he didn't reply, Tolland spoke again.

"I'm serious."

"Okay."

"And as for this, we can talk another time, if you want."

"Now's all right."

"You're sure?"

"Yeah."

"Okay, then. Have you heard your friend Sonny Beal and his father got arrested yesterday?"

"Jesus, no. What for?"

"Stealing stuff off boats, over to Campobello. There was a chase, and shots were fired. Somebody got hit."

"Holy shit. Is Sonny okay?"

"Oh, he's fine. It was their boat that did the shooting."

Tolland proceeded to lay out the details.

Sonny and his father had gone out in the predawn dark and made their way to the Canadian side of the bay, where they had anchored their own boat and then used a low-hulled rubber raft to sneak alongside several other vessels at their moorings and make off with navigational gear and tools.

It had happened before, and the Canadian fishermen had set up a quick-response harbor watch. Someone had spotted them, and by the time the two were back aboard their boat, a waterborne posse had mobilized.

The pursuers had sent up flares to help identify the fleeing craft, whereupon someone in it had fired a shotgun at the closest boat. One man had been hit, which had been enough to discourage further pursuit. But the Coast Guard and the State Police had already been alerted, and they had arrested the two when they tied up in Lubec, where they apparently were fencing the stolen goods.

Tolland shook his head and stared for a moment through the window to where the bay narrowed as it turned inland.

"Sad thing. His old man dragged him into something pretty god-damn serious."

"So what happens now?"

"Hard to say. The theft took place in Canadian waters, but the shooting seems to have been on our side. However it's handled, the Canadians will have to sign off on it, and you can bet they'll want some prison time."

"But just for his old man."

"Both of them is my guess. The guy who got hit may lose an eye. And as I said, it wasn't the first time."

"Who shot the gun?"

"Don't know yet. But that may not matter much. Once a gun goes off, things get pretty serious for everybody involved. You and I may see a young guy who just did what his SOB of a father told him to, but that's not the way the law sees it. Sonny's over eighteen, so in the eyes of the law, he's an adult who bears responsibility for his own actions, and he's gotten himself mixed up in something pretty bad. Which brings me to what I need to ask you."

Griff could feel his heartbeat in his throat, and in his ears, too, a thudding so loud it didn't seem possible Tolland couldn't hear it.

"I'd like to do this informally, just you and me talking. But you don't have to, of course. You've got a right to a lawyer."

Griff swallowed but couldn't chase the tightness from his throat.

"Are you . . . reading me my rights?"

Tolland smiled.

"No. You've been watching too much TV. Just trying to get a little information."

"I don't know anything about that stuff. Honestly."

"Nothing at all? He never mentioned anything?"

Griff shook his head.

"No."

"Did you ever get anything from Sonny that could have been stolen property?"

His forehead felt wet with sweat. He brought his hand up across it and through his hair, trying to make the gesture seem natural.

"No." There had been the digital recorder, but he'd made Sonny take it back. And anyway, it wouldn't be the kind of thing a fisherman would have. "Not that I can think of."

"Not as a trade for something or for you to sell for him or anything like that?"

"Nope."

"So there's not going to be anybody coming forward saying you two were selling any of the stuff they stole?"

"Selling it? Not me. Never. I swear to God."

Tolland nodded.

"Okay. Not that I thought otherwise, but in my job, you have to ask."

"Yeah."

"One more thing. We got a warrant to search their house, and one of the things we found in Sonny's room, tucked in the back of his closet, was a nice digital camera. The warranty folks say it belongs to you."

So Sonny had lied.

"Did you know he had it?"

"Yeah. I lent it to him."

"That's an awful nice camera to be lending."

"I guess. But we were pretty good friends at one time."

"Were? Not now?"

"We don't hang out that much anymore. Susan didn't like him."

"Why not?"

Griff smiled ruefully. "You want the whole list of reasons or just the top ten?"

Tolland chuckled.

"I think the biggest one was that her friends thought Sonny was a creep, and she didn't like having to explain why I hung out with him."

The chief reached into his pocket for a piece of gum.

"Want one?"

"No, I'm good."

"So you quit palling around with him?"

"We still did some stuff, but not as much."

"You remember when you lent it to him? The camera, that is?"

Were there photos? If so, they'd have digital date stamps.

"It must be a couple of years."

"And you didn't want it back?"

"I'd sort of forgotten about it. Once Susan and I got together, I kind of lost interest in photography. And anyway, my iPhone camera is really good, so I use that when I see something I want to take."

Oh God, he was speaking too fast, saying too much. He could see Tolland assessing him as he talked. He had to stop.

v . . ."

{ and tailed off.

..a ran his tongue around his gums.

"Why'd he borrow it?"

"We had a bet. He said he'd seen a great horned owl, and I said he was full of sh—that there weren't any on the island. He said he'd prove it by getting a picture."

"Did he ever produce the picture?"

"Nope. I don't think there's any around here, do you?"

"Not so's I've ever heard. But I don't think that's really why he wanted it."

Tolland didn't elaborate. Would it seem stranger to ask what he meant or to just let it go? He had decided it would seem weird not to ask when the chief spoke again.

"Old Sow's roaring."

He gestured toward the water, where one of the world's largest whirlpools formed each day just off the tip of Deer Island. The cross-currents of colliding water were swirling hard back on themselves, their tumbling white ridges outlining the huge circular torrent of treacherous water.

"I come down here a couple of times a month just to watch. You ever been out in a boat near it, Griff?"

"Nope. You?"

"With the Coast Guard a time or two. That's some current. Not enough to touch their cutter, but pretty damn strong, just the same. Back in the sailing days, it claimed quite a toll, or so they say. Took down a two-masted schooner once. Even now, with engines and all, you'd be surprised how many get caught up in it."

"Seems like it'd be easy to avoid."

"Doesn't it, though? And yet somehow, even knowing the danger, they get pulled into it. Sometimes they run out of gas. Other times, they shut down to fish, and the next thing you know, the current's got them, and they flood the motor in their panic to get going. And then they're in a real mess."

The chief looked straight at him.

"Sort of like life, in a way. You can just kind of float along, not paying any mind to anything, and the next thing you know, you've drifted into trouble. Happens quite a bit in small towns like this. I've seen some pretty good kids get into something that screws their life up but good."

"Like Sonny?"

Tolland shook his head.

"Sonny didn't drift; he got dragged into it by his worthless old man."

The chief's eyes held his for a moment that grew to a half a minute before he spoke again.

"So no, not Sonny."

Another minute passed in silence.

"Well, I've taken enough of your time. Where can I drop you?"

"Back by my truck would be good."

Tolland started the cruiser and put it in gear.

When they came to Griff's vehicle, he slowed and pulled to the curb.

"Keep your chin up, Griff. Things'll get better. If they don't, you call me, okay?"

"Okay." He opened the passenger door and got out.

Tolland started to pull away, then stopped.

"I forgot to ask—did Sonny ever admit defeat in the search for the great horned owl?"

"No."

"How much was the bet?"

"Not a lot. Twenty-five bucks, I think."

"You won't get it now. But I'll see to it that you get your camera back."

"Thanks, Chief."

"You take care."

"I will."

"I hope so, Griff. I really do."

CHAPTER 55

HE ANSWERED HIS cell without checking, thinking it was probably his father, who sometimes called when an urgent fuel request had come in after the dispatcher had left for the day. Now that autumn had arrived in earnest, people were discovering they had let the season catch them with nearly empty tanks.

"Hey, Griff."

"Sonny."

"How ya doin'?"

"Okay. You?"

As soon as the words were out of his mouth, he realized how stupid they sounded.

"Pretty much fucked, actually. Can you meet me somewhere?"

"You in town?"

"Just for a while."

"I've got a ton of deliveries."

"Don't worry, I'm not on the run."

"I'm just really busy."

"It's important."

"You got a car?"

"Yeah."

"How about Gleason's, six-ish?"

"See you there."

He rode out a little early, did a slow loop of the dirt road that traced the shore, and pulled off into the high grass over where the clearing gave way to the woods. A solitary boat plied the waters, beating its way through a sharp chop that ran with the wind and tide, the bow spray rising above the standing shelter in periodic bursts.

The water sustained everything here, drove what there was of an economy, brought what tourists came, and yet he could count on one hand the times he'd been out on the bay. He wondered if the fishermen felt more alive, more centered in what they did.

A few months ago, it had seemed as though his life was beginning in earnest. His life with Susan. Now his connection to things was measured in little more than the short length of hose he unreeled to fill the tanks of his father's customers. He couldn't bear the thought of doing it through another gray fall, another dark winter.

He'd been sitting there for five minutes when a silver Nissan Sentra swung into the clearing. A half a minute later, it nosed in beside him, and Sonny lowered the window.

"Hey."

"Hey."

"Like I said, I'm not on the run or anything. The judge gave me a couple days to get my shit together."

"I didn't know they did that."

"When you cut a deal. But he's got me wearing an ankle bracelet."

"What then?"

"Two years."

"Jesus. That sucks."

Sonny forced a laugh.

"You're telling me. But it's less than my lawyer said I'd get if the trial went the wrong way. And it's a hell of a lot better than eight to ten, which was what they offered the old man."

"He took it?"

"Yeah. They had us dead to rights."

"That's tough."

"Fuck him. He's an asshole—always has been, always will be."

"Where'll you go when you get out?"

"Back to Jonesport, I guess. My uncle—my mom's brother—is a carpenter. I'm hoping maybe he'll take me on."

"What about the detective thing?"

"Pipe dream, Griff. Probably always was, but definitely now." A wry grin crossed his face. "I guess I could open the 'It Takes a Thief' agency."

Both of them chuckled for longer than the quip merited.

"Time to let all that go. But I'll tell you this: I'm all done with him." He shook his head in contempt. "He wanted me to say I'd fired the shotgun. Said I'd get less time 'cause I was younger."

"Christ."

"It gets worse. He tried to get me to do it. When we were out there, I mean. Shoved the goddamn gun at me and told me to shoot at them. 'Aim right below their lights. We gotta back the bastards off.'"

Sonny lowered his head and coughed and looked away for a moment, then lit a cigarette and took a pull, holding the smoke deep before tilting his head and exhaling a long, thin plume.

"You know why I didn't?"

"Why?"

"Because I'd been thinking about Winters and . . . and that whole thing. That could have been the mother of all fuck-ups."

"Yeah."

"Thank God for Susan. Tell her I said so, okay?"

"We broke up."

"'Cause of that?"

"Pretty much."

"That sucks."

"Yeah."

"What'd she say?"

"That she doesn't know who I really am. And that I don't, either."

"Something to that, Griff."

"Not you, too."

"You know why I never told you about the stuff the old man and I were doing?"

"Because you're an asshole?"

Sonny eyed him with amusement.

"Because you're not. Because you're a good guy."

"She doesn't think so. Not anymore."

"Maybe she'll come around."

"I doubt it."

They fell silent for a moment, and when Sonny spoke again, he was on to something else.

"Winters keeping his mouth shut about it?"

"Seems to be."

"Wonder why."

"Maybe he meant what he said. About it being over."

Sonny took another drag and then tapped the cigarette out on the side of the car.

"You know about the camera, right?"

"The camera?"

"I had your camera. The cops found it in my room."

"I thought you left it in the woods, and somebody took it."

"Like you said, I'm an asshole. I wanted more pictures, and I knew you wouldn't go out prowling again. Anyway, the cops saw the ones of Megan. And some others."

"What others?"

"Probably better if you don't know. It didn't matter much, what with all the other shit they had on me. But I was thinking they might start coming after you, trying to make you a part of it."

"They haven't. Not yet, anyway."

"Well, just in case, I told 'em you didn't know anything about any of the shit I was doing, including the pictures. Not even Megan. So don't let 'em try some bullshit bluff."

"Thanks, dude." Griff let a moment go by. "So why'd you say you had the camera?"

"Like we decided. That I'd bet you I could get a picture of a great horned owl, so you lent me the camera, and I just never gave it back. I said I'd been out at night trying to get the shot, and that's how I got into the other stuff."

"What'd you say the bet was for?"

"Two hundred bucks."

"Two hundred? Who bets two hundred?"

"There had to be a good reason why I'd had it for so long."

"Makes sense. Thanks again for keeping me out of it."

"No problem. Hey, I got a six-pack here."

"Jesus, Sonny, you've got to be careful."

The familiar disdainful smirk came to Sonny's face.

"What, exactly, are they going to do, Dark Avenger. Toss me in jail? 'Oh, sorry, Judge Fuckwad, beat you to it. I'm already going.' The way I see it, I've only got a couple of days left, and I'm gonna enjoy myself. So, you want one?"

Griff shook his head.

"Suit yourself."

He wanted to get away, but he couldn't. Not yet.

"When I get out, maybe I'll give you a call."

It was hard not to say anything, but one conciliatory comment would lead to another. Sonny read his silence appraisingly.

"Not a good idea, I guess."

"Probably not."

"Because you're trying to get back with Susan?"

The out was there for the taking, but Griff shook his head.

"We need to move on. Both of us."

Sonny looked out over the water for a minute, then opened a beer and tilted it back.

"Can I ask you something, Griff?"

"Sure."

"We were real friends, right? I mean, it wasn't just because you could come over and drink and watch Megan?"

"Yeah, we were."

"Good friends?"

"Really good friends."

Sonny started to say something further but apparently thought the better of it. He raised his beer in a mock toast and drank again.

"Thanks."

"Right back at ya."

"Well, then, I guess that's it."

He reached forward and started the Sentra.

"Take care of yourself, Griff."

"You too, Sonny. You too."

He sat there for half an hour before heading back to town. What he'd said had been true.

And something beyond that. Sonny had been not just a good friend but his best friend—and in the end, a better friend than he himself had been.

CHAPTER 56

"OH MY GOD." The wineglass fell from his mother's hand and broke on the kitchen floor, shards scattering across the room. "When?"

"In Bangor. Last week."

"Last week? Why didn't you tell us?"

"I was waiting for the right time, Mom."

That was pretty much true. And tonight, with her cooking dinner in the kitchen and his father paying bills at the table, it had seemed like the appropriate moment.

But it was also because he had enjoyed carrying the secret around with him, knowing things were about to change abruptly even as everyone else thought life was moving to a placid and predictable beat.

"Griffin, you can't do this. You could die."

"I could die tomorrow, driving the oil truck."

"You know what I mean. And I couldn't bear it."

Tears were welling in her eyes, and he felt a twinge of remorse for having wondered if the dropped glass was simply drama.

"Mom, thousands of guys join up every year. Every month. Most of them come back just fine."

"They don't join up hoping to go to Iraq."

"Some do."

A tear spilled from her eye and ran down her cheek.

His father, lips pursed, looked from her to him.

"It just seems completely out of the blue, Griff. I think you should take more time to think it through," he said.

"It's easy to make an impulsive decision when you're unhappy, and we know how depressed you've been about Susan," she added.

"Grandpa served in Korea."

"That was different."

"Not really."

"And why Iraq? It's so dangerous. You could end up on the front lines."

"There aren't any front lines. We're on an advise-and-assist mission now."

"Well, you could still be seized by one of those radical groups. Or be hit by a roadside bomb." She dabbed at her eyes. "I always knew Bobby would leave, but I thought we'd have you here."

Her assumption that Bobby would go while he, of course, would stay somehow annoyed him.

"I need to go out and do something. The Army seems like a good place to start."

"I know this thing with Susan hurts, Griff, but there will be other girls."

"Mom, it's not like I have a death wish because Susan and I broke up. It just made me think about things. I want to serve—do my part."

"When do you go?"

"Next week."

"Oh, Griff, no." She looked imploringly at her husband. "Carl, can't you do something?"

His father came to her side and put his arm around her, then turned to him.

"If you join when you're in an unsettled state, they'll let you change your mind, Griff. They don't want people who don't want to be there."

"But I do want to be there. I'm pumped about it."

They surveyed each other for a moment in silence. Then his father nodded.

"Well, if that's really the way you feel . . ." He turned to his wife. "It's a big decision, Estelle, but it's his decision. And he's made it."

With that, he retrieved the broom and began sweeping up the broken glass.

CHAPTER 57

"AREN'T YOU GOING to open it?"

Dan had picked up the package at the mailroom, but then left it sitting untouched there on the table in the Bates Dining Commons.

"Not now."

"Why not?"

"Why?"

He couldn't explain to her that anything with an Eastport return address threatened to breach the mental wall he had built to keep at bay the welter of emotions and decisions that loomed in the middle distance.

Hannah's eyes narrowed, and a frown wrinkled her forehead. She put her hand gently on his arm.

"Dan, are you okay?"

"Yeah. Almost all better."

He had explained his injuries by saying that on the night of his mother's funeral, he had wandered up to the Battery Field and then to the top of the small monadnock that was one of Eastport's highest points, to look out over the town as he contemplated her life. And that as he'd turned to leave, his slick-soled dress shoes had slipped on the wet face of the rock, sending him sliding partway down its short southern slope.

"I gotta admit, the shoes aren't totally to blame," he'd said, affecting a rueful laugh. "I had some bourbon while I was sitting there. And then the pint broke and cut up my arm when I fell."

"That's so sad. You sound like old Eben Flood."

"Like who?"

She had tilted her head back and closed her eyes for a moment, then started to recite:

"Old Eben Flood, climbing alone one night
Over the hill between the town below
And the forsaken upland hermitage
That held as much as he should ever know
On earth again of home, paused warily.
The road was his with not a native near;
And Eben, having leisure, said aloud,
For no man else in Tilbury Town to hear:

'Well, Mr. Flood, we have the harvest moon
Again, and we may not have many more;
The bird is on the wing, the poet says,
And you and I have said it here before.
Drink to the bird.' He raised up to the light
The jug that he had gone so far to fill,
And answered huskily: 'Well, Mr. Flood,
Since you propose it, I believe I will.'"

A look of concentration flooded her face as she recalled the lines, and seeing her there, lost in the moment, her eyes intense, her dark, wind-tousled hair falling on her shoulders, he had felt a rush of elation. Here he was with a girl who could launch into a poem in a pizza place without being the slightest bit self-conscious about the turned heads.

"Wow," he said admiringly, "you English majors!"

"It's Edwin Arlington Robinson. Tilbury Town was his name for Gardiner, Maine, where he grew up. Anyway, he sits there drinking by himself and looking out at the town"—she paused and thought for a moment—"'where strangers would have shut the many doors that many friends had opened long ago.' It used to make me weep." She dabbed at her eyes. "But this is from thinking of you there, Dan, all by yourself. You should have called me *before* you left. I would have come with you."

But things between them had become increasingly strained since their happy reunion.

He hadn't said much about his trip, despite her many inquiries, and, regularly rebuffed, she had quit asking. On Thursday night, they ate together at the Dining Commons, a meal during which he had been mostly silent while she had made idle chitchat about campus events and then read him a witty poem she had written for her father's fifty-fifth birthday.

She was heading home the following morning to Andover, Massachusetts for the celebration, which was also the occasion for a mini family reunion that would bring a favorite aunt east from San Francisco. She had obviously labored over her poem, a send-up of her father's eccentricities delivered in unmistakable adoring-daughter overtones. It was full of puns and well-executed turns of poetic comedic phrases and would no doubt trigger waves of family hilarity, but it left him with a deep inner ache for the father, for the family, he had never had.

It concluded with a prediction that her father, when he gave his own remarks, would dissolve into the weepy sentimentality that regularly overcame him on family occasions.

> "Prove me wrong and you'll be owed
> This daughter's honest palinode
> But to earn that added serenade,
> You can't become a spring cascade.
> Be Attorney Hildreth of the stern court riposte
> And not Darling Dad, the lachrymose."

Hannah had looked at him, expecting a laugh, only to find him frowning and biting his lip.

"That bad?"

"No, no, it's good."

Now she frowned.

"Are you really okay, Dan?"

"Yes, really. I mean, I'm still kind of sore, but better every day."

"I mean okay emotionally. You seem depressed."

"I'm good."

"You don't seem good. Sometimes it's like you just kind of fade out of the moment."

"Like the Cheshire Cat?"

"I'm serious, Dan. I'm trying to help."

"You're not my shrink, Hannah."

"I know, but I really think you need to talk to somebody."

"I'm fine."

"It's not a big deal. Half of my friends have been in therapy. I've done it myself. It helps you understand yourself."

"I don't need help."

"Really? You've got a package, but you won't open it. Your mother died, but you won't let yourself grieve. I can't get you to say a thing about her."

He leaned back in his chair and locked his hands behind his head.

"Did you ever think that maybe, unlike you, I happen to be a private person?"

A hurt look transformed her face.

"I'm just trying to help."

"What would help is for you to back off a little. You didn't know my mother. You don't know how we got along. And you can't tell me what I'm supposed to feel."

She recoiled as though stung and stared for a minute out across the cavernous dining hall. Then, drawing a determined breath, she turned back to him.

"I'm sorry, Dan, but I can't be with someone who shuts me out when he's in pain—who lashes out when I try to get him to talk about it."

She was obviously expecting him to speak, but he didn't.

The silence between them grew steadily more oppressive until, tears spilling from her eyes, she got up and left.

CHAPTER 58

HE WAS LEAVING for basic training in the morning, and simply sitting around the house would make the evening hours interminable, so he decided to take a last drive around Eastport.

After a slow circuit through the sleepy downtown, then up Washington to High for a ride by the schools and through the cemetery, he drove through the North End and parked on the breakwater, out where he could watch the waves roll down the bay in the bright moonlight.

He'd heard from some of the former Eastporters who faithfully made the trip from Lewiston or Worcester or Springfield or Queens for the weeklong Fourth of July celebration that Eastport was one of the prettiest places anywhere. But how could you know until you'd actually seen something of the world? He doubted many of them had. Yes, they'd left, but mostly they'd gone somewhere to take a job or be near a spouse's family. Their distant domiciles lent their comments authority with the locals, yet he wondered whether they really knew even the region they'd relocated to, let alone anything beyond.

Some guys who had gone into the service came home every chance they had.

Not him. He'd use his leave to travel—first in the United States and then, once deployed, in more exotic locales.

He wasn't even worried about whether the other enlistees would like him.

"The Army molds you into a unit PDQ," the recruiter had said. "You're all in it together. There's no in-group or out-group, no jocks or preps or nerds or slackers or geeks or goths or emos or whatever else you have in high school these days. You go through basic training together, and you've got an instant bond. Once you're deployed somewhere, you depend on each other, and the people you depend on become your friends in a hurry. I know guys who've come back and started businesses together because they know they can trust each other, who've married each other's sisters, whose families go on vacation together every year. Ask anyone who's been in the Army, and they'll tell you the same thing."

What would it be like to have friends like that?

A car turned onto the breakwater. A Ford Focus.

He hadn't seen her since that afternoon at the community college. It would be too odd to encounter her this way, on his last night in town.

But it was Susan. She looked over and gave a tentative wave as she went by, then drove to the end of the pier and executed a U-turn. A moment later, she pulled up behind him, got out, and walked to his door. She was in a sage safari jacket he hadn't seen before, and her hair was styled differently.

"Griff, I really need to talk to you."

What if she's pregnant?

A wave of panic struck.

All his plans. Could she be? They'd been careful. But careful didn't always do it. Mistakes happened.

"Okay. You want to get in?"

"My mother heard that you've joined the Army," she said as soon as she'd settled into the passenger seat.

"Yeah."

"When do you go?"

"Tomorrow."

"So you weren't even going to tell me?"

Her distraught tone puzzled him.

"We haven't talked since . . . since that day."

"But this is different. It's so unfair. If something happens to you, I'll blame myself."

"Why?"

"Because you always said you wanted to stay here. Then we break up, and all of a sudden, you go off and join the Army. If we were still together, none of this would be happening, would it?"

"Probably not."

"What if you get sent somewhere dangerous?"

He thought about telling her but decided against it. The news would surely get out once he was there.

"You know that if something happens to you, it will haunt me forever."

"It won't be your fault, Susan."

"You just said you wouldn't have joined if we were still together."

Yet there was a distinction there, and suddenly, it seemed important to make her see it.

"But that doesn't mean it's *because* of you, Susan. After we broke up, I started to think about things—to try to figure out who I really am. I just can't see myself driving an oil truck until my father retires and then taking over the business."

At that, her look of agitation changed to one of uncertainty.

"I thought that was what you wanted."

"Only because I was scared, I think. Scared to go somewhere bigger, to try something different. Worried I couldn't make it. But you can't let fear rule your life."

The wind was shifting, and he watched a large breaker sweep obliquely toward the pier, piling onto itself as it raced along, an arc of spray rising after it hit.

"It's getting rough."

"Yeah."

They sat in silence for a moment, staring out at the waves.

"So what changed?"

He chewed his lip for a second.

"I don't know. Maybe just being on my own."

"So it's really not because of . . . us?"

"It's really not."

"Then I'm glad for you, Griff."

She fiddled with her bracelet for a few seconds.

"I've made some decisions, too, but they're pretty minor compared to yours."

"What?"

"I'm transferring to UMaine. In the fall."

"That's great, Susan." He let a sly grin come to his face. "Your mother must be happy. This spring is a twofer for her."

She chose to ignore his gibe and asked instead when he'd be back.

"Hard to say."

"But won't you get regular leaves?"

And so he explained his plan to use his time off to see the country and then the world.

They watched another breaker roll into the pier.

"Will you be on Facebook or Instagram or anything?"

"Nah. I can't stand that stuff."

"But you'll have e-mail, anyway."

"I don't know how that works in the Army."

"Well, will you write once in a while, just so I know how you're doing?"

He'd imagined this moment time and again since they'd broken up, imagined it from the riptide of despair to the sad but solid shoal of acceptance, and each time, he had luxuriated in his imagined response.

Susan, I'll be gone, and pretty soon, you'll be with some new guy who makes you laugh, and the last thing you'll want is some Army grunt sending you a mud-spattered letter from God knows where.

"I mean, only if you want to," she added.

"Sure."

A tear meandered down her cheek, and she smiled self-consciously as she wiped it away.

"I better say good-bye before I lose it. Take care of yourself, Griff."

She squeezed his hand and leaned a little forward, but he had looked down, and by the time he met her eyes again, the moment had passed.

"You too, Susan. You too."

Watching her taillights disappear, he thought of her question:

What changed? Which was her way of asking what had given him the courage to do it.

He could never have told her it was the moment in the cemetery facing Winters, the moment he had reached within himself and overcome his terror. The moment when he had pointed the pistol and fired the shot.

It was odd what came to define your life. Once he had realized Susan was there, once he had learned the truth about why Winters was looking for him, he had been overwhelmed with relief that no one had been hurt. And yet, in those seconds before, when he had seen Winters coming at him with something in his hand, everything had faded except for the realization that his worst fear was coming true—and that if he didn't stop Winters, no one else would.

Faced with that, he had pushed back the panic and found the self-control necessary to aim and shoot. And discovered something about himself, something he hadn't known was there.

How could you explain that to anyone? You couldn't. The greater truth of near tragedy would obliterate any lesser truths. So it would be his secret. It wasn't a proud secret, exactly. It couldn't be, given what it might have cost.

And yet, it wasn't shameful, either. His reality had been false, but the assertion of will, the mastery of fear, the execution of purpose— those were sure and solid things. Things to build a future on.

CHAPTER 59

HE SPENT ALL of Friday and most of Saturday in the Bates library, catching up on the reading he had missed while in Eastport. Both nights he returned, late and tired, to his room, threw himself down on the standard-issue dormitory single bed, and tried to take stock of things.

The package from Eastport sat there on his desk, still unopened, a memento whose mystery made him shudder. He couldn't imagine what was inside or who might have sent it, nor did he really want to know.

He tried Dr. Pratt's office three times on Monday morning before his call was finally picked up by the receptionist rather than the answering service.

"Is this an emergency?" she inquired when he asked it was possible to see the therapist that day.

"No. But can you tell him I really need to talk to him?"

At four p.m., he was reclined on the couch in the psychiatrist's office.

"So you don't want to tell her because you're afraid you'll lose her, but now you've lost her because you wouldn't tell her."

"Yeah."

Dr. Pratt frowned in thought.

"I wish you'd told me all this before."

"I hate talking about it."

"Yeah, I got that. Still, it explains some things about you, Dan. Not in a bad way, mind you." They sat in silence for a few moments, then he spoke again.

"When does the trial start?"

"Late August, early September, from what they say."

"So she'd find out then anyway."

He nodded.

"Yeah."

"And you're pretty sure it would scare her off?"

"I was. Like you said, now she's left."

"You can still tell her."

"It just seems easier to forget about everything until the trial's over and then move on from there."

"Without her?"

"I guess."

"But you care about her."

"Yeah."

"Do you love her?"

"I don't know what that feels like."

Dr. Pratt raised his tea and took a sip.

"Maybe because you've never let your guard down. And maybe, instead of getting on with your life once the trial's over, you'll just keep drifting along without ever giving yourself a chance to get close to anyone."

He ran the heels of his palms down his face. "So what would you do?"

"Doesn't matter. This is something you have to decide for yourself."

"But that's why I'm here. I can't decide."

"Well, here's how it looks to me. Growing up the way you did has made you self-reliant, but it's also closed you off. Now you have to decide whether you're confident enough in who you've become to let people you care about know the truth."

He couldn't find his Swiss Army knife, so he tore away at the brown packing tape with the point of a pen. When it gave, he opened the box and sorted through the crumpled pages of the *Banger Daily News*. The wadded newspaper protected a picture frame wrapped in tissue paper.

The photograph was of a headstone in the snow. CLARA WINTERS.

A foot or so in front of the engraved granite, there lay a single rose, its blossom a vivid splash of red against the pristine snow.

An envelope was taped to the back of the frame, and inside it, he found a clipping from the *Quoddy Tides* of the same photo.

"An unexpected spring snowstorm blankets the resting place of Clara Winters, where someone has left a fresh rose every few days since her death," read the caption.

A sheet of violet writing paper held a short note.

> Dan,
> I thought you might like the original photo. I hope things are good with you.
> Susan

He set the photo on his desk but then shook his head.

It was beautiful, the kind of thing you might linger over in a gallery, but too melancholy to contemplate every day. Wrapping the tissue paper carefully back around the frame, he slipped it into the bottom drawer, along with the note.

He stood and pulled on a fleece. The day had been mild, but there was a bite in the air now, and he was glad of the extra layer as he walked across campus.

It was later than he'd thought, and by the time he reached her dorm, the doors were locked. He stepped back from the building and looked up at the third floor. The light was on in her room, so he leaned against the nearby bike rack and waited. Ten minutes passed without anyone coming or going.

Finally, he reached for his cell phone. Her voicemail picked up after the fifth ring.

A woman approached, several books under her arm, and looked at him. He recognized her from geology class.

"Dan, right?"

"Yeah. Ginny?"

She nodded.

"Waiting to get in?"

"Kind of."

Fitting her key to the lock, she stepped inside and pushed the door back toward him.

"Thanks."

He started briskly up the stairs but paused at the second landing. He stood there for a moment, frowning, then turned and retraced his steps.

There was a bench outside perhaps twenty yards away on the green, and he sat down and called again. This time her phone went directly to voicemail. He ended the call and thumbed a text: "Hannah, I'm outside. Please come talk."

It was almost eleven now, and the night was getting steadily chillier. He sat and watched until her light blinked out, then walked slowly back to his dorm.

THE END

ACKNOWLEDGMENTS

I'd like to thank several people for their help with this novel. My wife, Marcia, a sharp-eyed but diplomatic editor, helped save things on a day when my recently completed draft seemed to have collapsed into warring-formats digital disaster.

Andrew Goldstein, author of *The Bookie's Son,* gave me a piece of invaluable advice that, once executed, got me several offers from publishers.

A lunch by the ocean with Islandport Press Editor-at-Large Genevieve Morgan, herself a writer, quickly persuaded me Islandport was the perfect publisher for this Maine story.

At Islandport, I was fortunate enough to work with writer and editor Ron Currie Jr., whose own novels dazzle. *Just East of Nowhere* benefited greatly from his perceptive reading and suggestions.

To each, my sincere thanks.

ABOUT THE AUTHOR

Scot Lehigh graduated from Shead High School in Eastport, Maine and earned degrees at Colby College and the University of Massachusetts at Boston. In addition to *The Boston Globe,* Lehigh has also worked as a reporter at *The Times Record* of Brunswick and *The Boston Phoenix,* where he was a Pulitzer Prize finalist. *Just East of Nowhere* is his first novel. He now splits his time between Cape Elizabeth and Boston.